A Sprig of Blossomed Thorn

Patrice Greenwood

Evennight Books
Cedar Crest, New Mexico

A Sprig of Blossomed Thorn
copyright © 2013 by Patrice Greenwood

ISBN: 978-1-61138-272-3

Published by Evennight Books, Cedar Crest, New Mexico, an affiliate of Book View Café

Publication team: Sherwood Smith, Nancy Jane Moore, Chris Krohn

A Sprig of Blossomed Thorn

Patrice Greenwood

in loving memory of

Rita A. Krohn

Acknowledgments

My heartfelt thanks to the following people for their invaluable assistance with this novel: to my publication team, Sherwood Smith, Nancy Jane Moore, and Chris Krohn; to Ken and Marilyn Dusenberry, Sally Gwylan, Kathy Kitts, Pari Noskin, D. Lynn Smith, and Jerry Weinberg for their thoughtful input, and to Chris Krohn for his untiring support. Thanks also to the members of Book View Café for their help with a thousand little details of bringing out a book, and to the founders and staff of the St. James Tearoom for inspiring me to write this series.

From the white-blossom'd sloe my dear Chloris requested
A sprig, her fair breast to adorn:
No, by Heavens! I exclaim'd, let me perish, if ever
I plant in that bosom a thorn!

—Robert Burns, "On Chloris requesting a sprig of blossom'd thorn"

1

"Was Captain Dusenberry married?" I asked as I filled Willow's cup with Keemun tea.

My guest used the silver tongs to pick up a lump of turbinado sugar and drop it carefully into her cup, then leaned back in her wing chair, stirring. "Oh, no. He died a bachelor. Very sad."

"I was wondering if he planted the wisterias."

"I doubt it, Ellen. They'd be gigantic after a hundred and fifty years."

"True. I hadn't thought of that."

She smiled slightly and sipped her tea. She was dressed in ivory silk, almost the same color as her hair, which was caught up in a French twist. She looked ethereal against the blue velvet of the chair, the opposite of the way I usually pictured her.

When I'd first met Willow Lane, owner of Spirit Tours of Santa Fe, the weather had been colder and she'd been dressed à la Santa Fe lady: black broomstick skirt, turtleneck, and boots, accented with a tasteful necklace of tiny bird fetishes. I'd been wary of her business and of the advice she'd offered, but in fact both had proved advantageous for me.

She had added Captain Dusenberry—the first occupant of the Victorian house that was now my Wisteria Tearoom—to her spirit tour, which meant that three times a week she brought a handful of curious visitors to the tearoom. Enough of them came back for tea that I could only be grateful to Willow. I'd invited her to have afternoon tea with me as a thank-you, and also because I wanted to pick her brain.

I offered her a plate of scones and lemon-thyme tea cakes. "I checked with the Preservation Trust, but their file doesn't have much about him. Will you tell me his story, or must I sign up for a tour?"

She laughed, a little musical chuckle, and added a tea cake to her plate. "I won't make you take the tour. I know you're a skeptic."

"I'm just not sure...."

"After almost three months? I assume the activity hasn't stopped."

I shrugged a shoulder and broke open a scone. "No, but there could be other explanations."

She didn't answer. I slathered clotted cream and lemon curd on my scone, ignoring her steady gaze. At last she set down her teacup and took a bite of the cake. "Mmm. Delicious."

"Thank you. The thyme is from my garden."

"I saw that you had planted herbs among the roses. Very charming."

"I like old traditions."

"So do I." She finished the little cake in one more bite and picked up her cup and saucer. "All right. The Dusenberry talk."

Willow took a sip of tea, then shifted in her chair, drawing herself up to speak. She was always poised—possibly a habit from her vocation—and her voice was soft and rich.

"Captain Samuel Dusenberry was the quartermaster at Fort Marcy Post from 1849 until April 5th of 1855, when he was murdered in his study."

In this house, I could hear her add, but she spared me.

"He was originally from Brooklyn, New York, and had been in the army since receiving his commission at the age of twenty in 1834. He was an exemplary officer and was buried with honors in the military cemetery north of Santa Fe."

I nodded. I'd visited his grave on more than one occasion. It was becoming one of the places I went when I needed to get away and think.

"Do you want to hear the details of the murder?"

I took a swallow of tea. "He was shot, I believe."

"Yes. In the back, twice, while he was seated at his desk. The killer was never found."

"Was it a robbery?"

"No. Nothing was taken from the house. The captain's body was found by his servant, Private David Rogers, on the morning of April 6th. The post doctor's report stated that the captain must have been shot the previous evening. The murder weapon was a Colt Navy pistol, a common sidearm at the time. One of the balls was found embedded in the wall of the study."

"Navy sidearm?"

"Military in general, though lots of civilians had them, too."

I gave a small sigh. "So there's no clue who killed him."

"It was probably a man. Probably someone he knew."

"What could he have done to make someone want to murder him?"

"That, I don't know." She sipped her tea, watching me over the rim of the cup.

Movement caught my eye and I looked up to see Rosa, my newest server, in the neighboring alcove, petite and pretty in her wisteria-purple dress and lace apron. She picked up a place setting from the low table and carried it to the Lily alcove at the front of the parlor.

"Well, thank you," I said to Willow. "Can you recommend any books that might mention him?"

"I don't know of any. My information came from the obituary and the post records. I didn't dig into his career before he came to Santa Fe. He'd been at Fort Marcy Post for six years."

Rosa returned to the Rose alcove next to where we were seated, put the place setting back where it had been, and stood frowning at it. I lifted the cozy from our teapot and freshened our cups.

"Was there a report in the newspaper?"

"Just a couple of lines about the investigation was all I found, other than the obituary. 'Anyone with information please come forward.' You could look through later issues to see if there's any more; I just checked the month after his death."

"I guess if there'd been more the Trust would have known about it."

"Not necessarily. It might be worth digging a little deeper. I could help."

"Would you? I don't really know where to begin."

"The state archives are a good place to start. The Museum of New Mexico might have something, too—they have a lot of the old records and artifacts from the military post. I can introduce you to one of the curators."

"Thank you, that would be great."

"My pleasure. I'm glad you're taking an interest in the captain."

Rosa picked up the place setting again and carried it back to Lily. I finished my scone and tried to ignore her; I would ask her what was up after my guest departed.

"How is your tour doing?" I asked, offering Willow a plate of sweets.

"Quite well, thanks. Business is up. Captain Dusenberry has brought out some repeat customers."

We chatted about her tour over strawberry meringue puffs, wisteria-blossom petits fours, and chocolate mousse cups. Willow was interested in offering a combination spirit-tour-and-tea package for the summer tourist season; she'd rearrange her usual tour so that the tearoom was the final stop, and her customers would have afternoon tea in the dining parlor that had once been Captain Dusenberry's study. I agreed to try it for the month of July.

The part of me that wanted to say "no" made a feeble protest, but I swatted it down. Regardless of my personal doubts and discomforts, I couldn't deny that Captain Dusenberry was good for my business, too.

When Willow and I were both sugared out, I flagged down Rosa and asked her to fetch a box for the leftover sweets, which I insisted Willow take home. I walked her to the front door and said goodbye on the *portal* with its wisteria-twined wooden columns.

They might not be over a century old, but the vines were still impressive, climbing up onto the *portal*'s roof and nearly reaching the upper-story windows of the old house. They were lush now that summer had arrived, heavy with leaves and the occasional cluster of pale purple blossoms giving off a heady perfume. A couple of bees drifted around the flowers.

"Thank you for a lovely tea," Willow said. "I'll call you about going to the museum."

"Yes, thanks. And thank you for the information about the captain."

"Any time. You know I'm glad to help." She gazed up at the wisterias as she said that, and I had the feeling she wasn't just talking to me.

I watched her walk down the path between my rosebushes, which were happily blooming in the June sunshine. I had planted them the previous fall, and they seemed to be enjoying their new home.

Going back in, I found Rosa clearing the dishes from the Iris alcove where Willow and I had been sitting. Confusing, having a server with a flower name, since I had named all the alcoves after flowers in a fit of romanticism when I was designing the tearoom's layout. I had needed to hire someone fast, though, and my chef, Julio, had suggested his cousin Rosa.

"Thank you," I told her. "You don't have to do that if you're busy."

Rosa shook her head, smiling. "Dee's got the party in Hyacinth, and that's it until four."

I nodded, picked up the tiered tea tray, and followed her back to the butler's pantry. I watched her long, black braid swaying as I tried to think of a way to ask what she'd been doing in Rose and Lily without coming across as a snoop.

I didn't know her well, yet. She'd only hired on two weeks ago, as a replacement for Vi, who had landed a summer job as an apprentice with the Santa Fe Opera.

Come to think of it, Vi had a flower name, too: Violetta. Her mother was opera-mad and had named her for the title character in *La Traviata*.

Vi was thrilled to death about being an apprentice, once I convinced her that I wasn't angry and she'd get her job at the tearoom back when the season was over. That had been a bit of a rash promise—my budget was tight as a drum--but I had hopes that business would increase enough by September to enable me to keep it.

We piled the dishes by the washing station, where Dee's brother Mick was gallantly working his way through the huge stack that had accumulated since the morning, bopping to the music in his earbuds. Everything about him was long—limbs, hair, fingers—but he was dextrous and always handled the fragile china with competent care. I gave him a smile and he nodded.

Rosa went into the butler's pantry and started to tidy. I strolled up front to the gift shop and looked at the reservation list. As she had said, there was one party coming in at four. They were assigned to sit in Jonquil, not Rose or Lily. Why the back-and-forth with the place setting, then?

A puzzlement.

Dee, one of those lovely young blondes who always look so fresh and pretty, stepped in from Hyacinth, a teapot in her hands. "Kris is looking for you."

"Thanks," I said, glancing at my watch, a gold pendant that had been my grandmother's and been left to me by my own mother.

I'd promised to meet with my office manager after my tea with Willow. Giving up on the puzzle for the moment, I hurried upstairs to Kris's office, which shared a doorway with mine.

The slanting roof made the upstairs rooms seem smaller than they actually were. Kris's desk was near the window, which was open to the gentle breeze. The floor creaked beneath my feet—a loose floorboard I'd been meaning to have fixed—but Kris didn't look up from her computer monitor. Unusual; she normally greeted me when I came in. I sat in one of her guest chairs.

She wore a baby-doll dress with a sweetheart neckline and little puffed sleeves, except it was black. It also had lacings all up the front. Her black hair brushed her jaw, the trimmed edge so perfect it looked knife-sharp. Her nails were polished in frosted white.

Kris's Goth styles actually suited the tearoom much better than I had expected at first, and she always dressed with care. Having seen what she wore when she was going out with her friends, I was grateful for the restraint she exercised in choosing her work attire.

I watched her, and she continued to avoid my gaze. I wondered if something was amiss or if she was just feeling especially Goth that day. I was tempted to ask, but didn't want to offend her. Though we worked well together, I was always conscious of the authority my being her employer gave me. We were close enough in age to make that feel a bit awkward, and I tried to be careful not to patronize her.

"Would you like some tea?" I offered.

"No, thanks," she said. "You must be floating by now. How was your tea with Willow?"

"Fine. She's got some interesting ideas that might bring us more business."

"Good." Kris glanced at me as she handed me a printed page. "Here's the adjusted budget for June."

I looked at the page. Business was up, but so were expenses.

The tearoom was picking up steam as the summer tourist season in Santa Fe came into full swing. The murder that had occurred there in April was almost forgotten, except by a few people who thought it fascinating and came to visit the tearoom regularly on account of it, about which I could hardly complain.

We were busy every day and I would soon need to hire more staff, which was a mixed blessing. The budget was tight —scary tight—and most days I spent as much time in the office with Kris as I did downstairs in the tearoom with my customers.

"Is there any way we can hire another dishwasher?" I asked. "By the time Mick gets here things are stacked to the roof."

Kris shook her head and reached for her mouse, twitching it across the desktop as she gazed at her monitor. "Another part-timer is too much. Mick's not working forty hours, though. You could see if he's willing to come in an hour earlier. Would that help?"

"Anything would help! What about two hours earlier?"

"That would kick him to full-time. Do you want to give him full benefits?"

I bit my lip. One thing I'd insisted on was that my full-time employees—Julio, Kris, and now Rosa—have decent health care benefits. I subscribed to a plan through the chamber of commerce. It was expensive, but I felt strongly that offering good benefits would increase the loyalty of my staff. I only wished I could offer health care to the part-timers as well—all of my servers were part-time except for Rosa—but at this stage it just wasn't feasible.

"Let me talk to him," I said. "Maybe we'll try an hour earlier for now."

"OK."

We moved on to review my chef's orders for next week. Expensive as well, but good food required good ingredients and I wasn't about to scrimp. The Wisteria Tearoom was already enjoying a reputation for high quality and I had no intention of cutting corners. I approved Julio's list.

"Anything else?" I asked.

"That's it for now."

I paused, hoping Kris would say something about whatever was making her frown, but she kept her attention on her monitor. "All right, thank you, Kris. I'll be downstairs if you need me."

She nodded absently, pale fingernails gleaming in a ray of sunlight as she danced her mouse again. I left her to her numbers.

Wanting to spend some time outdoors, I paused to fetched my shears and a broad-brimmed straw hat from a closet above the stairwell. The closet and the tiny bathroom beside it were on my list for a remodel; both were old and in need of updating, but they'd have to wait until the tearoom's cash flow improved.

Downstairs, I stopped in the pantry to grab a vase and fill it with water, then stepped into the kitchen to talk to Mick. He was open to coming in an hour earlier, nodding enthusiastically at the suggestion. Maybe he would use the extra income to actually paint his '77 Mustang a single color.

Not that I minded it; he parked it in back of the kitchen, so no guests could see it even from the dining parlor.

I went out into the garden and sighed with pleasure at the scent of the roses in the afternoon sun. They were mostly hybrid tea roses, with a few floribundas and one wickedly-expensive David Austin, a Wildeve, that I'd placed at the southeast corner of the front *portal*. Planning and planting the rose garden had been therapeutic for me as I grieved for my father, and now that they were in their first full bloom, I was glad that I'd invested the time and money.

Setting the vase at my feet, I began clipping blooms, inhaling each one's perfume before slipping it into the water. Some were spicy, some lightly sweet, some as rich as chocolate.

Their colors were delicious, too, ranging from palest pink to the flamingo-hued Tropicana to deep velvety red, and beyond. Peace roses in multicolored pastels. A Sterling Silver, almost the same hue as the wisterias. I smiled, gazing over my garden as I clipped one of the lavender blossoms, pleased that my vision had become reality.

I paid for my inattention. Drawing my hand away from the bush, I caught the back of it against a thorn and yelped.

I switched the rose to my other hand and sucked at the puncture. Stupid; should have worn my gardening gloves. They were for grubbing in the dirt, though, and I hadn't wanted to wear them with my nice tearoom dress.

I had too many faces, perhaps. Gardener, manager, hostess —not to mention the times when we were so busy I had to step in and help the servers. There had been a week, right after Vi was accepted at the opera, when I'd spent a lot of my time in the butler's pantry.

Ah, well. I loved it all. The tearoom was worth all the effort I'd put into it so far, and I knew it would only get better.

I clipped another half inch off the stem of the Sterling bud I had cut before adding it to the vase, then went inside to wash my little wound and comfort myself by arranging my cut roses.

2

The next morning I was at my desk when Kris came in to work. She headed straight into her office without pausing to say hello.

I was sure there was something bothering her. I stood, went to my credenza and picked up a tall Russian tea glass containing a mixed half-dozen of the roses I'd cut the day before, then went to the open archway between our offices and knocked on the sill.

"Good morning. I cut some roses for your desk."

"Thanks," she said without looking up as I set the flowers in front of her. Her outfit today was a black lace dress with tight-fitting long sleeves and a spray of velvet violets at the point of a rather plunging neckline.

"Want some tea?" I said.

"No thanks."

"Sympathy?"

That got her to look up, at least. "For what?"

I shrugged. "Anything. I'm a good listener, you know."

Her skeptical look softened and she glanced down. "I know."

I kept silent, waiting. She blinked a couple of times, then reached for her mouse. "I have to get these bills entered."

I suppressed a sigh. "OK. If I can help with anything, let me know."

"I will."

I went out to the hallway, rubbing the back of my hand, still sore from the rose scratch. Warm light glowed through the window at the west end of the hall. Soon it would start getting hot upstairs in the afternoons; I needed to think about some thermal drapes, but they'd have to wait.

I went downstairs to the butler's pantry, where Dee and Rosa were preparing tea trays for our first guests. Dee had her blonde hair up in a knot on top of her head, a style she'd adopted as the weather got warmer. It made her look sweetly innocent, though in fact she was the most intellectual employee I had, next to Kris. We traded "good mornings" as I passed through on my way to the kitchen.

Julio was dancing to salsa music and working at the long prep table in the center of the kitchen. He wore his usual plain t-shirt over loud, baggy pants—tropical fish, today—and a matching baker's cap that didn't quite restrain his wild black curls. He had cucumber sandwiches laid out on the table in long rows, and was garnishing each with a dab of herbed butter and a sprig of fresh dill.

"You could have the girls do that, Julio," I said, stepping to the window and lowering the volume on the boombox.

"Girls are too busy," Julio said, his face set in artistic concentration. "Rosa keeps running back and forth to Lily."

I turned to look at him. "Why?"

Julio grimaced. "Abuela's coming."

"Your grandmother?"

He nodded. "The matriarch."

That might explain Rosa's odd behavior the day before. I glanced toward the pantry but didn't see her.

"Shall I help?" I asked Julio.

"Not now. Maybe in a bit."

I resisted the urge to pick up one of the sandwiches and instead snagged a bit of trimmed crust from a plate Julio had set aside. The orange I'd had for breakfast wasn't holding me.

I popped the crust in my mouth and left him to his work, going into the butler's pantry to scare up some tea. The girls, bless them, had a pot of Assam under a cozy in the far corner of the pantry. I poured myself a cup and added a splash of milk.

Dee glanced up at me and smiled. I smiled back, then stepped down the hall toward the front parlor to look for Rosa.

I found her in Lily. Usually she wore her hair braided, but today she had it loose, caught back from her face in a barrette. She was straightening the place setting on the low table and glanced up as I came in.

"Good morning, Rosa."

"Morning, Ms. R.," she said, sounding slightly nervous.

"Ellen, please." I glanced at the table set for one. "Special customer?"

"My grandmother's coming. I've been telling her about the tearoom and she finally decided to come."

I smiled and sipped my tea. "That's wonderful! I look forward to meeting her."

Rosa straightened the spoon beside the teacup. "I was going to put her in Rose, but then I thought she'd like to look out at the garden."

"Absolutely."

Rosa bit her lip. "Maybe I should switch her to Rose, though."

Aha.

"Well," I said, "This is one of our prettiest views, and the roses are blooming like crazy."

"Yes. She loves roses," Rosa said. "They're her big hobby. She's in the Rose Guild. That's why I couldn't decide."

"Well, Rose doesn't have a window. Would she enjoy the name more, or the view?"

Rosa smiled. "The view. You're right, I'll leave her here. I just want to make sure today is special for her. She hasn't been very well lately."

"Oh, I'm sorry to hear that."

"She fell and broke her hip a few months ago. She's just starting to go out a little again."

"Well, we'll make sure she has a wonderful tea. If you know of anything she'd especially like, tell Julio. He can probably whip it up."

"She'll love everything." Rosa smiled brightly. "Thanks, Ms. R.—Ellen. I guess I'm just a little nervous."

I patted her shoulder. "Don't fret. She'll have a lovely time."

I had finished my tea. Leaving Rosa to perfect Lily for her grandmother, I went back to the kitchen and set my cup and saucer on the windowsill, out of the way.

"Julio, you know those rose petal jam sandwiches we've been talking about?"

"Mm-hm." He was still garnishing, and didn't look up.

"Why don't you whip up a couple for your grandmother? I'd like to do something special for her."

That made him look up. "You know her?"

"No, but if my grandmother was coming to tea, I'd want to give her the royal treatment."

He tilted his head, thinking. At first the hard line of his jaw made me think he was about to refuse, then his face relaxed. "Yeah, OK. After I get the brioches in the oven."

"Why don't you let me finish garnishing those sandwiches, so you can get started on the brioches?"

He handed me the sack from which he'd been piping herbed butter. I set it down to wash my hands and put on an apron before working with the food, then covered and put the trays of finished sandwiches in the refrigerator to make room for Julio to work. While he wrapped tidbits of brie in puff pastry, I finished garnishing the sandwiches and got them all into the fridge, ready to be placed on tea trays just before serving.

"Where's the jam?" Julio asked as he slid a tray of brioches into the oven.

"In the pantry. I'll get it."

I fetched a jar of the rose petal jam I'd made a few days earlier and gave it to Julio, then hurried out to the garden to clip a red rose to use for garnish on the sandwiches. A bush of peace roses caught my notice, the perfume from their blooms filling the morning air. I clipped a handful of them, too, and took them inside.

Rosa passed me in the hall and I stopped her and offered her the peace roses. "Pick a vase and put these in it, then put them in Lily for your grandmother."

"There's already a vase of roses there!"

"I know, but you can never have too many. Careful—I didn't trim the thorns," I added as Rosa reached for the roses.

She took them gingerly and held them to her face. "Mmm. They smell wonderful! Thanks, Ellen!"

"You're welcome."

I took the red rose to the kitchen and washed it, then pulled off the petals and put them in a small bowl. Julio had already mixed some of the rose petal jam with soft butter and spread it on a slice of thin, white bread. He spread more jam on another slice, then put the two together and cut three small rounds out of the sandwich with a cookie cutter. He garnished each with a red rose petal and arranged them on a small plate.

"Bueno?" he asked, glancing up at me.

"Bueno. Thank you, Julio."

"De nada."

I put the rose sandwiches in the fridge, then took the rest of the petals to the pantry, adding them to the larger bowl of rose petals the girls were using to decorate the tea trays. Glancing at my watch, I saw that it was almost time to open.

I took off my apron and went up to the gift shop to check the reservations sheet. Party of one in Lily: Maria Garcia. Two other parties were coming in at eleven, when we opened. By noon all the seating areas would be full, even the dining parlor, which was booked for a bridal shower.

I made the rounds, checking to make sure everything was in place. The lights were on in the dining parlor. I hadn't done it, and my first thought was that Captain Dusenberry was at it again.

Or it could have been one of the girls, getting a head start on setting up for the bridal shower. I left the lights on and went to the kitchen to deprive Julio of his salsa music. He took it philosophically, donning a pair of ear buds and switching to the music player in his pocket when I turned on the house stereo.

String quartet music began to play softly throughout the tearoom. In the pantry, the girls were busy brewing tea and setting up the tiered trays of food for the first customers. I took down a teapot to make tea for Kris and myself.

"There are some rose petal sandwiches in the fridge for your grandmother, Rosa."

Her face lit with a surprised smile. "Thank you! You didn't have to go to all that trouble!"

"It's no trouble. Julio and I have been talking about adding them to the menu, so this will be a test. Let me know how she likes them."

"I will."

"Kris was looking for you," Dee said, glancing up at me.

"Is she downstairs?"

Dee nodded as she set a dish of lemon curd on a tray. "In the front parlor, last I saw."

"Thank you."

I set the tea to brew, then hurried to the parlor and found Kris standing in Lily, gazing out the front window. The wisteria vines cast a deep shade on the west-facing *portal* in the morning. Beyond them, the roses glowed in the sunshine.

"Dee said you were looking for me," I said.

Kris jumped slightly, then turned from the window. "Yeah.

Got a call from Johnson's. The cream delivery's going to be short next week."

"Oh, no! What happened?"

"They had a spoiled batch, had to throw it all out. Two days' worth."

"Ouch. Are we going to get anything?"

Kris nodded. "Half what we ordered."

I bit my lip. We used fresh local cream to make our clotted cream, no small feat at over a mile above sea level. Julio had spent weeks perfecting his recipe.

"We'd better call Hooper, then." Hooper Dairy was all organic and charged accordingly, but they were my best fallback when Johnson's couldn't fill our orders.

Kris nodded. "How much should I ask them for? The full difference?"

"Let me check with Julio." Movement outside the window caught my eye, a trio of ladies in summery dresses coming up the path to the tearoom. "I'll be upstairs in a few minutes, after we open. Oh, I brewed us some tea."

We went back to the butler's pantry where I gave her the teapot, then Kris headed up to her office while I went to open the front door and greet the waiting guests. I showed them in and got them seated, then returned to the front door.

As I opened it to greet the ladies, my gaze slid past them and caught an unusual sight. A van from El Vaquero restaurant, one of my many competitors, was parked by my front gate.

3

The van's driver, an Hispanic man of about forty, came around to the passenger side, took an aluminum-framed walker from the back and set it up, then helped a frail-looking, elderly Hispanic woman out of the front seat. This must be Julio and Rosa's grandmother.

Suddenly the van made sense. I remembered from Rosa's employment application that she had previously worked in a New Mexican restaurant, though I had forgotten which one. It appeared she had stronger ties to the place than I'd known.

I hurried out and down the path to open the front gate, smiling at the Hispanic lady. "Good morning! Are you Mrs. Garcia?"

She looked up at me as she leaned on the walker, dark eyes bright and curious, a lopsided smile of amusement on her wrinkled lips. She was dressed in Sunday best, a flowered dress with lace trim at the collar and cuffs, and modest jewelry glinting at her ears and neck. Her hair, black with a peppering of white throughout, was freshly coiffed. Clearly she'd taken pains to look nice for her solitary visit to the tearoom.

"Yes," she said in a voice rather stronger than I'd expected.

"I'm Ellen Rosings. Welcome to the Wisteria Tearoom."

"You're Rosa's employer." Her voice was slightly slurred, making me wonder if she might recently have suffered a stroke. Rosa hadn't mentioned it, if she had. Perhaps it was just general frailty, after her injury.

"That's right," I said. "We're very glad to have Rosa here. Won't you come inside and make yourself comfortable?"

She smiled. "Thank you."

I held open the gate while she slowly pushed the walker through it. The Hispanic man who had driven her hovered anxiously in her wake. Something about his jawline—firm, determined—made me think he resembled Mrs. Garcia.

Rosa came running down the path and confirmed my suspicion by giving the driver a hug. "Thank you, Papa!" she said, then turned to Mrs. Garcia. "Thank you for coming, Nana!"

Mrs. Garcia paused to receive a dutiful kiss on the cheek from Rosa. "Gracias, hija. You can go, now, Ricardo. Thank you for bringing me."

"Have a good time, Mama." He kissed her on the cheek as well, then watched her continue up the path toward the tearoom under Rosa's escort. "What time should I pick her up?"

"We like to allow our guests plenty of time to relax and enjoy themselves," I said. "Between twelve-thirty and one would work, but isn't that your lunch rush?"

I nodded toward the restaurant logo painted on the van. He glanced at his wristwatch.

"Yeah. And I've got to get back."

"You're the owner of El Vaquero, aren't you?"

"Manager. Mama still owns the place." He stuck out a hand. "Rick Garcia."

"I'm pleased to meet you," I said, shaking hands. "I love your rellenos."

His brows rose a little. "Thanks. So, I'll come back at one."

"Could Rosa drive her home?" I suggested. "It would save you a trip."

"No, no, I don't want her skipping work."

"She can stay a little late to make up for it."

He paused and gave me a long look. "That's nice of you. Gracias."

I smiled. "De nada."

He flashed a brief smile in return and climbed into his van. I hurried back to the tearoom, where Rosa was settling her grandmother in Lily.

The third party scheduled for eleven o'clock arrived shortly thereafter, and I had my hands full for a few minutes. When I finally had a moment to look in on the seated guests, I found Mrs. Garcia sipping tea and gazing out the window.

"Your roses are very lovely," she said, glancing up at me.

I smiled. "Thank you."

"The leaves are a little yellow on that Grande Dame. You might want to give it some iron chelate."

"I just gave it some last Sunday, actually. Rosa tells me you're a gardener."

"I like to grow roses, yes. I have been a member of the Rose Guild for twenty years," she said proudly, almost defiantly.

I smiled. "Well, I'm nowhere near so experienced. I appreciate your advice."

"If you want to learn about growing roses, join the Rose Guild." She smiled. "You'd be welcome there."

"Thank you. I'll consider it."

She lifted her cup and saucer, and her hands shook so much that the china clattered. Weathered hands, spotted with age. She ignored their shaking and with slow determination raised the teacup to her lips.

I noticed a bandage hidden by the lace cuff of one wrist, leftover from an IV, perhaps, from when she'd been in the hospital with her broken hip. I felt deeply sorry for her, and at the same time I admired her courage. To stay active in the face of such physical challenges was no mean feat.

Rosa came in with a three-tiered tea tray of savories, scones, and sweets, scattered with rose petals, and placed it on the low tea table before her grandmother. Mrs. Garcia carefully put down her cup and clasped her hands.

"Oh, it's so beautiful!"

I couldn't help feeling a little swell of pride. We work hard to make the trays beautiful, and always hope for just this kind of reaction.

"These are rose petal sandwiches," Rosa said, pointing to the little rounds on the top tier of the tray. "Ms. Rosings had them made specially for you."

Her grandmother's bright eyes fixed on me. "That's so kind of you! Thank you."

"My pleasure. Enjoy your tea."

I slipped out, leaving Rosa to explain the menu—and probably to serve her grandmother—while I looked in on the other customers. Everything was going smoothly, so I snatched the opportunity to consult Julio about next week's cream and run upstairs to tell Kris to order just two extra gallons from Hooper.

By the time I got downstairs again, three women carrying beribboned gift bags were waiting in the hall by the front door. They were the first of the bridal shower guests, slightly early for their reservation. I escorted them back to the dining parlor, then stepped across the hall to the butler's pantry where I found Dee and Rosa starting to set up the next trays.

"Bridal shower's here. Go ahead and make them some tea."

Dee nodded and took down two large teapots, handing one to Rosa. I took down a pitcher and began filling it with ice from the pantry's refrigerator.

"How's your grandmother, Rosa?"

She smiled. "Fine. She loved the rose sandwiches."

"Good."

I filled the pitcher with filtered water and a couple of lemon slices. Returning to the dining parlor, I found that two more of the bridal shower guests had found their way in and were chatting up a storm with their friends. I began filling the water goblets on the table, but before I had gone halfway around it the chandelier flicked off and on.

Conversation stopped. I glanced up at the chandelier, thinking, *Not now, please!*

It turned off again, then on after two seconds, then flashed three times in fast succession.

"What is that?" said one of the shower guests, staring at the lights.

"Old wiring," I said, smiling. "So sorry."

I put the water pitcher on the sideboard and hurried out into the hall. Captain Dusenberry was usually discreet, and didn't disrupt my business. This, though, was more than he had ever done before. If he had done it.

I felt a cold dread, standing in the hallway, looking around for whatever had awakened the Captain's attention. I tried to tell myself it really was just old wiring, but my gut disagreed.

"What is it?" I said softly.

The sound of hasty footsteps made me turn. Rosa had come out of the front parlor. She saw me and ran down the hall toward me, her face streaked with tears.

4

"Rosa! What's the matter?"

I caught her in my arms and she gave a sob. "M-my grandmother!"

"Come here."

I pulled her into the little hallway outside the restrooms, where there was a chaise longue. Taking out my handkerchief, I dabbed at her face with it, then pressed it into her hands.

"Stay here. I'll go and see."

Rosa sobbed into the handkerchief. I left her sitting there and hurried to Lily.

Mrs. Garcia was slumped in her chair, tea spilled across her lap and the cup fallen onto the floor. I gazed at her, breathing hard, trying to decide what to do. At best she was unconscious. At worst...

I stepped forward and took hold of her wrist. It felt frail, with no pulse that I could find, though I'm certainly not an expert. I tried her throat with no more success. Gently, I shook her by the shoulder.

"Mrs. Garcia?"

No response. My heart sank. I took her teaspoon and held it before her nose. No misting of breath on the silver. Carefully, I set the spoon down on the table.

Another death in my tearoom. Even if it proved to be natural causes, it would not look good.

I swallowed, knowing I had to call for help, dreading the chaos that was about to return to my beautiful, peaceful tearoom. I went out to the gift shop and called 911.

The dispatcher assured me a team of paramedics would

arrive soon. There was little more I could do, but I returned to Lily.

Remembering the way the police had invaded the dining parlor a month ago after one of my guests was found strangled there, I pulled the pocket doors closed and loosed the drapes at the window. It would at least keep curious eyes from staring into Lily.

I looked back at poor Mrs. Garcia. I wanted to pick up the teacup, set things to rights, but instinct warned me not to touch anything. I shouldn't have picked up the spoon, though it hardly mattered. My fingerprints on a teaspoon in the Wisteria Tearoom were anything but unusual.

Returning to the hall, I found a young couple waiting there, along with four elderly ladies in red hats. One of them, a tiny woman sporting a purple feather boa along with her wide-brimmed picture hat of bright scarlet, was all too familiar.

I managed to summon a smile. "Mrs. Olavssen. I didn't know you were coming in today."

She blinked and tilted her head in the way that reminded me so of a bird. In fact, I still thought of her as the Bird Woman.

"Yeah," she said. "We've formed a chapter of the Red Hat Society."

"So I see. You all look stunning. Why don't you step into the gift shop while I look up where you'll be sitting today?"

I smiled at the young couple to let them know they were included in the invitation, and they all followed me into the gift shop. At the podium where we keep the reservation list I picked up the phone, dialing Kris's desk.

"Kris, can you come downstairs and help for a few minutes? We're a little swamped. Thanks."

I hung up and checked the reservation list. The couple were to sit in Hyacinth, one of two small seating areas just off the gift shop. I showed them to it, then gritted my teeth and led the Red Hat ladies to their reserved area across the hall—in Jonquil, right next to Lily. I was doubly glad that I'd closed the pocket doors.

"Oh, the garden looks so pretty!" exclaimed one of them as she sat facing the window.

"Thank you. I'll go check on your tea," I said, anxious to escape.

"Can we get some champagne, yet?" said the Bird Woman, plopping herself down on the sofa.

I shook my head. "I'm sorry, our wine license still hasn't been issued."

"Too bad. We'll just have to come back."

I smiled again and slipped out, glancing toward Lily on my way back to the hall. My instinct was to try to keep things going, try to preserve normality despite having a dead woman in the front parlor. It would all fall apart shortly, but for now I felt I had to keep up the facade.

Down the hall I saw Dee cross from the dining parlor to the butler's pantry, casting me a harried glance as she went. A moment later Kris came down the stairs.

"What's the matter?" she asked.

"Can you help Dee? Rosa needs some quiet."

"Sure," she said, glancing toward the pantry.

"Come up front. We've got people coming in for the bridal shower."

I led her to the gift shop, which I was grateful to find empty of guests. In a low voice, I briefly apprised Kris of the situation.

"I'm going to take Rosa upstairs," I said. "She's very upset."

"I'm not surprised. Don't worry, I'll hold the fort."

"Thank you. Call me when the paramedics—"

A burst of sirens sounded from the street outside. We both glanced toward the front windows, and saw a full-length ladder truck pull up at the curb. Exasperated, I watched two paramedics climb down from it while an ambulance parked behind it.

I looked at Kris. "Are you all right with taking them to Lily?"

Kris nodded. I had a fleeting thought that she might even get a kick out of it, then banished the unworthy suspicion.

"I'll be right back," I said, and hurried out to collect Rosa.

She was trying bravely to stop crying, without much success. I took her upstairs to my office, where there is another chaise longue and more privacy, and settled her there with a cup of tea.

"I should call my father," she said, sniffling.

"Wait until we hear what the paramedics say. I'll go down and find out. Will you be all right here?"

Rosa nodded. I gave her shoulder a squeeze, then hurried back downstairs.

Kris was gone, though I could hear her voice along with a man's voice from the front parlor. Two bridal shower guests stood just inside the front door, looking hesitant and a little worried.

"Good morning," I said, smiling. "Let me show you to your party."

"Is something wrong?" one of them asked, glancing toward the parlor.

"One of our guests has taken ill, I'm afraid," I said as I led them down the hall. "An elderly lady. She's being taken care of. Here you are."

I opened the door to the dining parlor and saw them in. With luck, their friends would distract them from the paramedics. Closing the door gently, I glanced in the pantry and saw Dee putting hot scones on two tea trays decorated with ribbons of peach and turquoise, the bride-to-be's colors.

"Let me help you." I pulled on a plastic glove and started moving scones to the second tray.

"What's going on up front?" Dee asked.

"Rosa's grandmother fell ill."

"Oh. Poor Rosa!"

"We'll have to carry on without her, I'm afraid. Kris came down to help."

We carried the tea trays across to the dining parlor, where they were greeted with applause from the shower guests. I left Dee explaining the menu and stepped back into the pantry to check what needed doing next.

Tea was brewing for the couple in Hyacinth and for the Bird Woman's party. I put the couple's pot on a tray and took it up to them.

As I was coming out of Hyacinth I heard the front door open and close. I felt a momentary desire to run and hide rather than face another bewildered guest, but I straightened my shoulders and put on a smile as I stepped into the hall.

It was not a tea guest who had come in, but a man in jeans, leather jacket, and motorcycle gloves. I stopped short, blinking in surprise as my gaze met that of Detective Antonio Aragón.

5

"What are you doing here?" I exclaimed.

My heart had jumped on seeing Tony Aragón, for two nearly opposite reasons. The first was a natural dismay on having a police detective in the tearoom, particularly since he had been in charge of investigating the murder that had happened here on opening day. The second reason was that he was very attractive, which I knew was dangerous for me.

He shoved his hands in his jacket pockets. "Unofficial visit. I heard the dispatch call and thought I'd drop by to see if you needed any help."

"Oh. Well, that's very kind of you. The paramedics are there." I glanced uncertainly toward the parlor.

"Mind if I go in?"

I gave a helpless shrug, and started to lead him into the parlor. Kris came out of Lily and closed the pocket doors behind her, then stopped short on seeing Tony.

"Oh!"

"You remember Kris, my office manager?" I said.

Tony nodded. "Yeah. Hi."

A slight flush came into Kris's cheeks, and she glanced down. "Hello. Please excuse me."

She stepped past us, going out into the hall. Tony looked at me and I gestured toward Lily. He pulled open the doors and went in, and I followed.

Lily was a mess, cases of medical equipment lying open on the floor and torn plastic packaging everywhere. The paramedics had moved Mrs. Garcia to the floor and apparently tried to revive her, but they were no longer working on her. One of them was putting away a piece of medical gear, and the other was talking on his portable radio.

Tony stepped over one of the cases and looked down at Mrs. Garcia. He glanced at the nearer paramedic, who shook his head.

I bit my lip. Tony squatted down to look at the body, then stood up and glanced around the room. His gaze came to rest on the tea tray.

"Be a good idea to bag up that stuff, just in case."

I stepped toward him. "Surely it was natural causes," I said in a lowered voice. "She was very frail."

"Just in case," Tony repeated, pulling a pair of latex gloves and some plastic evidence bags out of another pocket.

So much for an unofficial visit.

I was annoyed, but I knew I was also generally upset, and that I shouldn't be quick to take offense. Tony meant well, and he was right. If any questions arose about the tea or the food, having them preserved would make everything easier.

I watched him pick up the teacup and ease it into an evidence bag. He did the same with the small plate of half-eaten food and the silverware, and slid the saucer into a third bag, then stood frowning at the tea tray.

"Do you need to take the whole tray?" I asked.

"No, but I should take the food."

"Shall I get you a take-home box?"

He must have noticed the edge in my voice, because he gave me a sharp glance. "Yeah. Thanks."

I stepped through the pocket doors and nearly collided with the Bird Woman, who had emerged from Jonquil. She jerked her head toward Lily, causing the red feathers on her hat to bob.

"What's going on in there?" she asked loudly.

I slid the doors shut behind me. "I'm afraid one of our guests took ill," I answered, keeping my voice almost to a whisper.

"Did she croak?"

Knowing it could only get worse, I ignored the question. "Please excuse me," I said, and hurried out.

I went to the butler's pantry and found Kris frowning at a large teapot. "That's for Jonquil," I said. "I hope it hasn't brewed too long!"

I pulled out the infuser and poured a little into a tasting cup to check. Not too strong, and it hadn't gone bitter or stewy. I set the pot on a silver tray and covered it with a cozy.

"Could you take it to them, Kris?"

"Sure." She picked up the tray and started out, encountering Dee in the doorway.

"I can take that," Dee said.

"No, you finish the trays for Jonquil and Hyacinth," I told her. "I'll be right back."

I grabbed a take-home box, and also a plastic container and lid in case Tony wanted to take the tea that was in Mrs. Garcia's teapot. I had no time to be upset at the moment, but I knew that later I'd need fifteen minutes of privacy in which to freak out and then consume mass quantities of chocolate.

I followed Kris back to the front parlor. A woman and two pre-teen girls, all in dresses and summer hats, were waiting in the hall.

"We'll be right with you," I told them, then hurried into the parlor.

The Bird Woman was still standing outside Lily, eavesdropping on Tony and the paramedics. Regular customers are bread and butter to an establishment like mine, and they must be treated like royalty, regardless of whether they might be a trifle odd. I smiled and gestured toward the tray Kris was carrying.

"Here's your tea!"

The Bird Woman looked Kris up and down. "Wow, that's a

hot dress! You should have all your girls wear that," she said to me. "You'd get more men in the place."

Kris and I traded a glance, then she stepped into Jonquil. The Bird Woman followed her, for which I gave silent thanks. I went into Lily and gave Tony the box and container.

"Thanks," he said, taking out his cell phone. "I better call someone to collect this stuff. I can't take it on my bike."

"I could have someone drive it to the lab, or wherever it needs to go," I offered.

Tony shook his head. "No. Have to maintain a chain of custody once it's taken into evidence. Thanks, though."

The paramedics had packed up their cases and now started out with them. Remembering the party waiting to be seated, I hurried after them. The mother looked rather alarmed at the sight of the paramedics trooping out.

"Thank you for waiting," I said, shutting the door behind the men. "Please come into the gift shop while I look up your reservation."

They were scheduled for one of the front parlor seating areas, but I decided to switch them to Marigold, in the back parlor behind the gift shop. It had a window overlooking the rosebushes on the south side of the house, and no view of the street. I made a note on the reservation list and saw them comfortably seated, then hurried back to the pantry.

"Iris is here, but I put them in Marigold," I said to Dee.

"Oh. OK." She peered at the schedule taped to the pantry's refrigerator.

"I'll take Hyacinth's tray. How's the shower going?"

"Fine. How's Rosa's grandmother?"

I couldn't speak, could only shake my head. The hysteria hovering in the back of my mind threatened to come forward, but I fought it down, then picked up Hyacinth's tea tray and carried it out.

The paramedics had returned with a stretcher. I waited for

them to pass, then delivered the tea tray to Hyacinth and returned to the front parlor.

One of the paramedics looked at me and gestured to an urn of flowers on a pedestal. "We'll have to move this."

I picked up the urn and stood aside while they set down the stretcher, moved the pedestal, then picked up the stretcher again and carried it into Lily, pushing the screen aside. I put the urn back on the pedestal and followed them, wondering if I should call Rosa down to say goodbye to her grandmother.

No. That's what funerals were for. But I would have to go up and give her the bad news.

"Dang!" said Bird Woman's loud voice behind me. "Hope it wasn't the cucumber sandwiches!"

6

I turned and saw the Bird Woman peering into Lily. I couldn't get to her at the moment, which was probably fortunate. My way was blocked by the stretcher which now bore Mrs. Garcia's body, tactfully covered with a blanket. The paramedics eased it out of the parlor and I hurried past them to open the front door. I had half-expected more disruption than they'd actually caused, and was beginning to hope that my patrons would be able to enjoy their tea after all.

But what if it *was* the sandwiches?

No, it couldn't be. Our food was completely fresh and of the highest possible quality. I'd watched Julio making the sandwiches myself.

I'd also eaten some of the scraps.

Brushing aside doubt, I saw Kris returning with the tea tray for Jonquil and followed her. The Bird Woman and her friends were standing at the window, watching the paramedics take Mrs. Garcia away.

"Wouldja look at that!" said the Bird Woman to her friends. "Last time somebody croaked here I didn't get to see it!"

"Your food is here, ladies," I said brightly.

"Just put it on the table, honey," the Bird Woman told Kris. "We'll get to it in a minute."

"Shall I explain the menu?" Kris asked, glancing doubtfully at me.

"Nah, I know what it is," said the Bird Woman, standing on tiptoe to peer over one of the crosspieces of the window. "Already had it once this week."

Kris and I withdrew, knowing when to accept defeat. I

returned to Lily, where I found Tony picking up the bits of plastic wrapping the paramedics had left behind.

"You don't have to do that," I said, reaching for them.

"Figured you'll probably be needing this space." He glanced at his collection of evidence bags and containers. "Um, do you have a bag or a box I could put these in?"

"Of course."

I took away the trash and returned with a wisteria-colored shopping bag from the gift shop. Tony gazed at it briefly, then shrugged and started loading his evidence into it.

"I'll get the china and silver back eventually, I hope," I said.

"Yeah, you will. Probably sooner than later. Hey, don't worry. This is just a precaution."

He glanced toward the window as a police squad pulled up outside. The ambulance was already gone. I hadn't noticed its departure.

Tony picked up the shopping bag, then looked at me. "You OK?"

I nodded. "Yes. Thank you for stopping by."

"You know, anyplace where a lot of older people come this is going to happen. The casinos get one or two a month, seems like."

I smiled. He'd meant it to be comforting, but I found the thought of coping with dead customers on a regular basis to be rather distressing.

He was still gazing at me, dark eyes intent. "Should I call you, later?"

My heart gave a little jump. I nodded. "Please do, especially if you hear any news."

"OK."

We went out to the hall, passing Kris who was showing a newly-arrived party to their seating. Tony paused by the front door, giving me another long look. Finally he smiled and squeezed my upper arm, then went out.

I stood in the open doorway, watching him stride down the path to meet the policeman at the squad car. My arm tingled slightly where he had touched it, and I absently rubbed it.

Why, I wondered, was I so strongly attracted to him? He wasn't at all the sort of person I ordinarily spent time with.

He liked motorcycles and rock music. I liked china and lace and Mozart. I spent my days creating a delightful place for people enjoy a quiet cup of tea, while he devoted his to resolving some of humanity's uglier problems. He did clean up quite nicely, though, when he cared to make the effort.

I watched him get on his bike and leave, followed by the squad car. A moment later a sedan parked at the curb and three ladies got out.

More customers. Time to get back to work. I closed the door and glanced into the front parlor, then into the gift shop where I found Kris looking over the reservations list.

"Kris, can you hold the fort a little longer? I need to go talk to Julio and Rosa."

"Sure." She gave me a somewhat doleful look. "Give Rosa a hug for me."

I nodded. Bracing myself, I walked back to the kitchen.

Julio was taping a note to the door of the oven. The kitchen was clean; he'd shut down for the day. He looked up as I came in.

"The last batch of scones is in the butler's pantry."

I nodded. "Julio, I have some bad news."

He straightened, turned, and stared at me. "Abuela?"

I nodded.

"That's what the sirens were."

"Yes."

"Is she dead?"

I swallowed the sudden tightness in my throat, and nodded.

He stood very still, blinking. I found my voice.

"I'm so sorry, Julio. They said it might be a stroke."

He nodded.

"You don't have to come in tomorrow."

"Yes I do. You need me."

"We can manage, if..."

"I'll be here."

He went into action suddenly, grabbing his music player, his thermos, jacket. I watched him head for the back door like he needed to escape.

"I'll be here," he said again over his shoulder. The screen door banged behind him.

I took a deep breath, then went upstairs and found Rosa in the hall, sitting by the front window where I had placed a couple of chairs overlooking the garden. She stood up as I approached.

"I heard the sirens..."

"Rosa, I'm so sorry."

"She's dead, isn't she?"

I nodded. Rosa nodded, too, and raised my handkerchief— which was quite soggy by now—to her eyes. She dabbed at her face, then broke into fresh sobs. I gathered her into my arms and let her cry.

"Take the rest of today off, and tomorrow, too," I told her when the bout of tears had subsided. "Do you want me to drive you home?"

"N-no, I can manage."

"Would you like me to call your father and let him know?"

She hesitated, then nodded. "If you don't mind."

"Of course not," I said, though it wasn't a call I looked forward to making. "Go on home, then. Take care of yourself."

"Thank you, Ms. R."

I walked downstairs with her and saw her off. Kris was straightening Lily, and together we returned the pedestal with the flower urn to its normal place. I walked into the alcove and stood looking around.

All trace of the tragedy was gone. Fresh place settings already gleamed on the table, awaiting the next customers. The fragrance of the peace roses hung in the air.

On impulse I stepped to the window and opened it a little, letting in a warm breeze, letting out the spirit of the departed, if indeed she was still here. I didn't remember where I had heard of that, but it seemed to make sense at the moment.

I said a silent prayer for poor Mrs. Garcia, and for Julio and Rosa and all their family. A sad day for them.

For me, the day was still full of obligations. I closed the doors to Lily and went out to meet them.

First order of business was the call to Rosa's father. I went up to my office for that, and fortified myself with a cup of tea before calling El Vaquero. I spent a couple of minutes on hold until Mr. Garcia came to the phone.

"This is Rick."

His voice sounded brusque, the voice of a restaurant manager whose hands were full. I wasted no time, getting straight to the point of my call.

"Mr. Garcia, it's Ellen Rosings, from the Wisteria Tearoom. I'm afraid I have bad news for you. Mrs. Garcia took ill during her visit here this morning."

"Mama's sick?"

"I called emergency, but the paramedics weren't able to help her. I'm afraid she died. I'm terribly sorry."

"Died?" He sounded stunned.

"Yes. The paramedics said it might have been a stroke. They left a number for you to call."

I read it to him and offered to help in any way I could. The silence on the line was heartbreaking. I knew I had ruined his day.

"I sent Rosa home," I told him. "She can take as much time off as she needs."

"Oh. Thank you."

"I'm so sorry, Mr. Garcia."

"Thanks. Thanks for calling."

His voice sounded broken as he said goodbye and hung up. I put down the phone and finished my tea, wishing I could have offered more comfort, but of course, nothing could change the awfulness of losing a parent, as I knew all too well.

I went back downstairs, and remained there the rest of the day. With Rosa gone I was shorthanded, and it being a Friday, we were booked solid until closing time at six. Kris stayed late to help, bless her. By the time the last customers left with their take-away boxes in hand, I was exhausted.

Kris came downstairs, carrying her black shoulder bag and a small shipping box. I looked up from locking the front door.

"Is that the samples from Empire?"

Kris glanced at the box and shifted it, tucking it more tightly under her arm. "No, it's something I ordered for myself. You said it was OK to have things sent here."

"Of course." I smiled. "Thanks for staying, Kris. You were a huge help today."

She smiled back. "No problem. Do you need me tomorrow?"

"Yes, if you don't mind. I told Rosa to stay home."

As she turned away I started for the gift shop to cash out the day's receipts from the register. The sound of a heavy tread on the front *portal* stopped me. Someone tried the front door, then a moment later pounded on it.

The front door is solid oak, surrounded on the top and sides by the small, single-paned windows called lights that one finds in older houses. I opened it to Tony Aragón, his jacket slung over one shoulder. His black t-shirt had a bosun neckline that showed a nice glimpse of his shoulders.

He smiled and gave an upward jerk of his head. "Hi. I was in the neighborhood, so I thought I'd just stop by instead of calling."

"Come in."

I opened the door wider and he stepped inside. Kris had wandered back, but now she turned away again.

"What's in the box?" Tony said.

Kris paused and glanced back at him. "Just something I ordered."

"Can I see?"

She turned and faced him square on, holding the box protectively. "Not unless you have a warrant."

7

My heart gave the little lurch that hits me whenever I'm in hostess mode and disaster threatens. I stepped between Tony and Kris.

"It's been a long day. Would you like some coffee, Detective?"

Tony shifted his gaze to me. "Thought coffee wasn't allowed in this joint."

"You know very well that it is, I just don't brew it during business hours."

The aroma of coffee is out of place in a tearoom. I had laid down the law on that early on. Julio always brewed two pots of coffee first thing in the morning and poured one into a thermos to drink during the day.

"Good night, Ellen," Kris said, and with a defiant glance at Tony, she headed for the back door.

"Good night," I called after her.

Tony was watching her narrowly. I waited until she was gone before offering a gentle reproof.

"I know it's your job to be inquisitive, but perhaps that should be left to business hours as well."

He looked at me. "I got no business hours."

"But is it appropriate to demand to look at someone's personal possessions when she's not suspected of anything?"

He glanced toward the back door again. "I was just curious. Recognized the shipping label."

That gave me pause, and also aroused my curiosity, but I had no intention of intruding on Kris's privacy. She was gone, so the point was moot in any case.

"Would you like that coffee?"

Tony looked at me. "Actually, I was going to offer to buy you a drink."

He said it flatly, and stared at me flatly. Had I been unacquainted with him I would have been taken aback, but I knew him well enough to know that this was defensive behavior, caused by a momentary lack of confidence. I smiled.

"That would be lovely. Let me just make sure everything's locked up. It's been a very long day."

He followed me as I made the rounds, turning off lights and checking doors. "Did the press come and hassle you?" he asked.

"No, thank goodness! I don't suppose they'd be that interested in the quiet death of an elderly woman."

"Maria Garcia was pretty important, actually. What you'd call a pillar in the Hispanic community. Fairly rich, too."

I turned off the lights in the butler's pantry and stepped back into the hall. "Was she? I know that she owned El Vaquero."

"And three other restaurants in town."

"Goodness! I had no idea."

I went into the kitchen to make sure the ovens were off. The note Julio had taped to the door of the regular oven said: "Don't Touch! Meringues." I left it alone and turned out the lights, rejoining Tony in the hall.

"I remember when I was a kid going with my mom to church so she could help decorate the altar," Tony said. "Maria Garcia would bring armfuls and armfuls of roses. Every Saturday, all summer long. What I can't figure is what she was doing in your tearoom," he said.

"Why shouldn't she come to tea?"

He smiled wryly. "No offense, but it's such a white lady thing."

I bristled. "I've had any number of Hispanic customers."

I knew I was overreacting. The truth was that he was right —most of my customers were Anglos, and most of them women. The exceptions were far in the minority.

"There was an added reason for Mrs. Garcia to come," I admitted. "Her grandson and granddaughter both work here."

Tony's brows rose. "Oh. Were they here today?"

"Yes. Her grandson is my chef, and her granddaughter was waiting on her. I'm afraid it was Rosa who discovered she was dead."

"That's rough."

"Yes. I sent her home. That's why it was such a long day for me—I had to fill in."

"Then you definitely need a drink. Got a favorite bar?"

I looked into the dining parlor, now restored to order after the successful bridal shower. I turned out the lights.

They came on again. Giving up, I closed the door and turned to Tony.

"How about the Ore House?"

He made a face. "Touristy."

"Good margaritas, though."

"You like margaritas?"

"Sure, when I'm in the mood."

He grinned. "What about tequila shooters?"

It was my turn to make a face. "No, thanks. I prefer grown-up limeade."

He laughed, which lit up his face, which gave me a shiver. His eyes are quite beautiful when he's not in cop mode.

"OK, how about Del Charro?" he said.

"Fine. Shall we walk?"

"It's kind of warm. We could go on my bike."

I glanced down at my lace dress. "I'd have to change."

To be honest, I wasn't anxious for a motorcycle ride. Not my favorite activity. I was about to suggest that I drive us instead, but was stopped by the long, appraising look Tony gave me.

"I'm in no hurry." He smiled lazily, and suddenly the thought of sharing the motorcycle seat with him had more appeal.

"OK."

I looked down the hallway, darkened now except for the evening sun coming in the lights around the front door. I couldn't really ask him to wait in the tearoom. It just seemed awkward to leave him downstairs.

"Um, come on up."

I led the way up to my suite, which occupies the southern half of the upper floor. The last time Tony had been in my private rooms he'd brought two cops and a search warrant, and had tossed the place pretty thoroughly. Remembering it reawakened my annoyance, and I had to remind myself that he'd only been doing his job.

I gestured to the two chairs and low table that make up what I generously call my living room. "Have a seat. Would you like a glass of water?"

"Sure, thanks."

Tony looked around as if he hadn't seen the place before. I suppose he hadn't, from an aesthetic point of view. Like the offices across the hall, it had a sloping ceiling and a chimney dividing the space east and west. I'd done my best to make the odd space cozy. The deeper, richer colors of the Renaissance decor in my suite were a departure from the Victorian frou-frou of the tearoom.

Tony nodded toward the brocade draperies caught back with tasseled cords that divided the sitting area from my bedroom. "This is different."

I stepped over to the kitchenette and fixed him a glass of ice water. "Yes, well—all Victorian all the time would get a little boring."

"And here I thought you couldn't get enough lace."

"Lace has its place." I handed him the glass. "I'll just be a minute."

I went into my bedroom and loosed the drapes. From my dresser I took out a pair of jeans and a casual top, and from my wardrobe a pair of sandals.

I changed, trying not to think about Tony being just a few feet away beyond the drapes, trying not to imagine him watching me undress. I failed at that, I confess.

I hung up my dress and tossed stockings and slip in the wicker basket I use for a laundry hamper. A glance in the mirror told me my hair needed attention, so I went back out, smiling at Tony as I passed him on the way to the bathroom. He was looking through one of my food magazines, but glanced up to smile back at me.

I took down my hair from its Gibson-girl do and brushed it out, then pulled it back into a ponytail. A touch-up to my makeup, and I was ready to face the motorcycle.

"OK," I said, returning to the living room. I picked up my purse and slung it over one shoulder.

Tony stood up and gave me another appraising glance, then grinned. "Nice. Didn't quite escape the lace, though." He flicked a finger across my shoulder, brushing the narrow band of lace that trimmed the neckline of my top.

I tilted my head, looking up at him. "Sorry about that."

"Don't be."

We went downstairs and I locked up the tearoom behind us. Hot sunshine hit us as we stepped off the *portal*, and the heady scent of roses filled the garden. I strolled with Tony down the path to the street, content to be just Ellen instead of Ms. Rosings, the Tearoom Proprietress.

We reached Tony's bike and he handed me his helmet. I shifted my purse strap to lie across me before putting it on.

"Aren't there helmet laws in this city, Mr. Detective, sir?"

"Yeah. I'll have to buy you one of your own, I guess."

"I don't know that it's worth that investment." I looked at the bike, having second thoughts.

"Don't worry. There isn't a cop in town who'll stop me for helmet violation when I've got a hot babe on the back of my bike."

I felt myself blushing, so I pulled on the helmet. Tony swung his leg over the bike and invited me to sit behind him. I swallowed, telling the butterflies in my stomach to go away, and climbed on.

The ride to Del Charro was tame compared to my first motorcycle adventure with Tony. I was pretty sure he'd been testing me on that occasion. Today he seemed more interested in reaching his destination. Even so, I held tight to him, both arms around his waist as he negotiated Santa Fe traffic.

He parked the bike and we walked into the bar, which was pleasant with dark wood everywhere and already crowded. Luck got us a table by one of the open windows overlooking Alameda Street, windows that went almost to the ground and perpetually stood open, making me wonder how often patrons simply stepped through.

Across the street was the little park where the Santa Fe River runs through its arroyo whenever there's rain, and a bridge where Don Gaspar Avenue crosses the river. People were strolling along the sidewalk, enjoying the summer evening. A couple of kids stood on the bridge, peering over the edge in a vain attempt to spot water in the riverbed below.

Tony ordered margaritas, giving the waiter precise instructions on what should go into them. I was amused to discover that he was an aficionado, even if it was of tequila. We nibbled on chips and salsa while we waited for the drinks.

"Any news?" I asked.

"News?"

"About Maria Garcia."

"Oh. Yeah, a little. The M.E. ruled out stroke. Thinks it might have been, uh—Somebody's Syndrome."

"What about the food?"

"It was delicious."

"Ha, ha."

He grinned at me. "It's in cold storage at the lab. No need to test it unless something suspicious turns up. We'll just hold it a couple of days until there's a solid diagnosis, then you'll get your china back."

"Thanks."

Talking about Mrs. Garcia, even tangentially, had brought back the sadness of the day. I caught myself wondering how Rosa and Julio were doing, and gazed out the window at the people in the park. Life going on, as it always did, though somewhere a family was grieving.

The margaritas arrived in two metal shakers, with tequila-marinated lime halves in each glass. Tony made a ceremony out of squeezing the lime into the glass, then pouring margarita over it. I did the same, and he raised his glass, offering a toast.

"Here's to the weekend."

"Amen," I said, lifting my own glass. I licked the salty rim and sipped. Cold, sweet and tart, with a powerful underlying punch of alcohol.

"Mmm, this is good. What kind of tequila is it?"

"El Tesoro añejo. Get the silver if you're drinking it straight."

"Oh, I won't be, don't worry." I took another sip and sighed with pleasure. "My weekend doesn't start for another day, actually."

Tony shrugged. "I don't really have weekends."

"Really? You just work all the time, like the cops on TV?"

"Pretty much. I've got so much vacation and sick leave piled up it's not funny."

"How come you don't take some time off now and then?"

He shrugged again. "Don't know what I'd do with it."

I watched him take a long pull at his margarita. I'd wondered, of course, whether he had a girlfriend or more likely a dozen. This last comment seemed to imply he didn't.

"Maybe you could ride your bike up to Taos, or Angel Fire, up through the mountains. It's so pretty up there, and cooler this time of year."

"Be kind of lonely," he said, watching me over the rim of his glass.

"Not if you went with a friend."

I realized belatedly that he might reasonably assume I was implying he should invite me. Since I quailed even at riding with him across town, the thought of spending several hours on a motorcycle was horrifying. I backpedaled.

"I mean, you must know other people who have bikes, who'd like to do that."

It sounded lame even to me. Tony gave me a wry look and took another pull at his drink.

"Have you ever been up to Salman Ranch?" I said, grasping at straws.

"No."

"It's up by Mora. It's a big raspberry farm—that's where I get my berries. There's an old mill up there that's kind of interesting. It's a nice drive, and if you go in August or September you can pick your own raspberries."

I was babbling. To stop myself, I picked up my glass and took a swallow of margarita. I could feel the alcohol starting to hit me.

"I'll have to think about it," Tony said.

I was silent, trying to think of some other topic. Truth was, I was nervous, as nervous as Tony had been when he'd invited me for a drink. We hadn't done much socializing. We were still unacquainted, mostly.

And I liked him. I could understand that he didn't do much besides work. I was the same; I had thrown myself into the tearoom and not left much time or energy for anything else. Maybe once we'd been open a few months I'd be able to take more time for myself, but the truth was, I was glad to keep busy. It took my mind off of losing my parents. That had been almost three years ago now, but it still hurt.

"What's the matter?" Tony said.

"What?"

"You looked sad, all of a sudden."

"Oh. Nothing." I shook my head and smiled. "Long day."

I sipped my drink, aware of him watching me. I put the glass down, alarmed to see that I'd already consumed half of the margarita.

"How about—damn!" Tony pulled a phone out of his pocket and frowned at it. "Sorry, I gotta take this."

I nodded understanding as he stood up and went outside. At least he refrained from taking a cell phone call in the bar, a courtesy I wished more people would exercise. I took parsimonious sips of my drink and watched Tony pacing on the sidewalk at the corner while he talked on the phone. After a minute he came back in and stood by his chair.

"I'm really sorry, but I've got to go."

I smiled. "Duty calls. I understand."

He pulled out his wallet and dropped some money on the table. "I know it's rude—"

"Not to worry." I waved a hand in dismissal, then picked up my glass and saluted him with it. "Thanks for the drink. Think I'll finish it and walk home."

"You'll be all right?"

"It's just a few blocks."

"I'm sorry."

"Shh. It's fine."

He stood gazing at me, looking frustrated and slightly

anxious. "Let's try again, OK?"

I nodded. "OK."

He bent down, swiftly kissed my cheek, and strode out, leaving me breathless with surprise.

8

I sat very still for a long moment, then drained the last of my margarita. Outside a motorcycle fired up and roared away. I put the glass down carefully, fighting the feeling that everyone in the bar was staring at me. They weren't. It had just been a kiss on the cheek. No big deal.

Except my heart was pounding. I closed my eyes, trying to regain my composure. I felt very strangely as if I had been seduced and stood up simultaneously.

Get used to it, I told myself. *If you're going to get involved with a cop, this will happen a lot.*

I picked up Tony's margarita shaker. Still half-full. Tempting, but I decided against it. I'd had plenty of alcohol, thank you. I didn't often drink more than a glass of wine, and as I stood up my head swam a little, confirming that I'd made the right choice.

The waiter was hovering a few feet away. I smiled at him to let him know all was well, then collected my purse and walked out.

The sun was close to setting. Shadows fell long across the narrow old streets of downtown Santa Fe, a city that had grown organically for the first two or three hundred years. Not many old buildings were left, but the new ones held to the strict code of John Gaw Meem's Pueblo Revival style, pale brown stucco and soft lines predominating.

I walked on the shady side of Don Gaspar uphill toward the heart of Santa Fe. Lots of tourists were out, still shopping or hurrying to dinner. I let the flow of foot traffic carry me as far as the plaza, then decided I wasn't ready to call it a night.

Taking out my cell phone, I sat on the flagstone-topped bench that surrounded the Civil War memorial in the center of the plaza and called my best friend Gina. If she wasn't out on a date, maybe she'd join me for a movie or a bite to eat. Eating would be a good idea, I reflected as I listened to the phone ring.

A light breeze stirred the leaves on the big trees in the plaza, throwing dancing dappled shadows on the ground. I was about to give up on Gina when she answered.

"Ellen! How are you? I've been thinking about you."

The bubbling cheer in her voice made me smile automatically. "I'm OK. I was wondering if you're busy tonight."

"Just doing laundry. Disgusting on a Friday night, isn't it? Want to rescue me?"

I laughed. "Yeah. How about dinner at my place?"

"Nope. My turn. I made a big pot of spaghetti sauce last night. Grab a DVD and come on over."

"Mine are all in storage."

"Then we'll stream one."

I looked at my watch. "I'll be there in about half an hour."

"Great! Ciao."

"Bye," I said, though she'd already disconnected.

I put away my phone and stood up to walk the two more short blocks to the tearoom. My head had cleared with the walking, and I felt safe to drive. Not bothering to go inside, I went around back to where my car was parked.

The sunlight had gone golden by now, and the east side of the tearoom was shadowed. Lights shone through the dining parlor's curtained windows, glowing on the hood of my car. Captain Dusenberry liked keeping the lights on in there a lot of the time, apparently. I'd resigned myself to the added cost on my electric bill.

The sun was setting as I drove to Gina's upscale condo in the southeast part of town. Her complex was built on a hillside and had great views and elegant, minimal landscaping. Modern lines but still brown stucco. A nice place, and on an advertising executive's salary, Gina could afford it.

She opened the door and immediately pulled me into a big, Italian hug. "Hi, girlfriend!"

Gina is good for my soul. I have a tendency to fall into melancholy now and then, and she snaps me right out of it every time.

She smooched me before letting me go. "Come on in while I finish the salad. This is going to be fun!"

I followed her to the kitchen, which smelled wonderful— garlic and herbs and savory tomato sauce. My mouth started watering. I picked up an olive from a dish sitting on the counter.

Gina was in casual mode, wearing a bright fuchsia tank top and white capri pants, both of which showed off her curvaceous figure. Her thick, curly, shoulder-length hair was tousled.

"Why aren't you out on a date on this fine Friday evening?" I asked.

"Why aren't you?" she retorted, chopping celery.

"I sort of almost was, but it got interrupted."

She raised a dark eyebrow. "Do tell!"

I explained about Tony inviting me for a drink and then getting called away. She listened, nodding sympathetically.

"He's that cute detective, right? You poor thing. You need a glass of wine." She took down a large, globe-shaped red wineglass and half filled it from a bottle that was already open on the kitchen counter.

"On top of a margarita? I don't know—"

"You're going to be here for a couple of hours, right? You'll be fine."

"I think I should eat something first."

"Good, because dinner's almost ready. Here." She handed

me the glass. "Take those olives and the bread out to the table. I'll be right behind you."

I left my purse in the phone nook and carried the food out to her dining room. Gina brought out the salad and a bowl of fresh-grated Romano cheese and went back to the kitchen. I wandered after her to fetch my wine, then returned to the dining room and stood sipping while I gazed out of the picture window at a peach-colored western sky. The sun was down, and a couple of small scraps of cloud caught its last bright gold gleams of light.

"I keep forgetting what a fantastic view you have," I said, turning as I heard Gina's steps.

"Yeah, me too." She set a huge bowl of pasta drenched in sauce in the middle of the table. "You see it every day, you start to take it for granted. Here's to remembering our blessings."

She raised her wineglass, and I joined the toast. "Remembering our blessings."

"Let's eat."

We sat down and didn't talk for a few minutes until we'd taken the edge off our hunger. I ate a piece of Gina's killer garlic bread and helped myself to a second, rationalizing that I needed it to counter the alcohol I'd consumed. I dished up a huge helping of salad to atone for the bread.

"So, I told you why I'm not on a date," I said, sprinkling cheese over my pasta. "Your turn."

"Oh, Alan had to work tonight."

I glanced up. "Alan? What happened to Ted?"

"Ted's history. Didn't I tell you about Alan? He's the catering manager at the Hilton. I met him when he came into the office a couple of weeks ago. Don't look at me like that! The Hilton isn't my account, so it's fine."

Gina went through boyfriends—if they could even be graced with the term—like a kid through a plate of chocolate-chip cookies. One right after another.

I sipped my wine. "So, Alan had to work."

"Some big event at the hotel, and he's short on staff."

"I know the feeling."

She gave me a curious look, so I told her about Mrs. Garcia and all of the chaos that had` followed. Her eyes widened as I talked.

"God, not again!" she said. "Did the press show up?"

"Not a peep from them, thank heaven, though Tony said she was pretty important in her own circles."

Gina frowned thoughtfully. "Garcia, you said?"

"Maria Garcia."

She nodded. "Yes, I've heard of her. She does a lot of charity work through the church. We're not in the same congregation, but I see her name in the newsletters. What a shame!"

"Yes."

I twirled some pasta on my fork, feeling a little down after recounting the day's woes. I'd probably be asked to attend a memorial service, I realized. And for Rosa and Julio's sake, I should go, if I could get enough staff in to cover the tearoom.

Staff—I'd have to sit down with the schedule tomorrow. With Rosa gone I'd probably have to redo the whole thing.

"Yoo-hoo. Earth to Ellen."

I glanced up at Gina. "Sorry. Thinking about work."

"Ah-ah, that's not allowed! Girls' night in, no work-think. Tonight is about fun and distraction."

"Yes, ma'am!"

Gina grinned as she stabbed at her salad. "Speaking of which, I got a flyer from the Santa Fe Institute. They're starting a new lecture series. First one's next Wednesday, want to go?"

"If I can. What's the topic?"

"Something about microbiology, I think."

"Hmm."

Microbiology didn't sound thrilling, but from past experience I knew that the Santa Fe Institute's lectures were always fascinating. They brought in great speakers from all over the country, and the house was always packed. Even Gina, who was not what I'd call deeply intellectual, enjoyed the talks, though I suspected it was partly as a chance to scope the crowd for potential future ex-boyfriends.

"So, the usual?" she said. "Lecture and dinner after?"

"If I'm free. I'll have to look at my schedule."

"OK, Miss Cautious. Hey, why don't you ask your detective friend, and I'll ask Alan?"

I took a sip of wine. "I'm not sure Tony'd be interested."

"Never know until you ask."

"True."

And I'd been mistaken about Tony before. I really shouldn't make assumptions about his interests.

My heart gave a flutter as I remembered his surprise kiss. He was interested in me, that much was clear. Would we get along despite our rather different backgrounds? Was it worth the effort to find out?

Miss Cautious. I deserved it, I admitted. It would be a dreadful shame, though, to let Miss Cautious become Miss Chicken. I might miss out on something really good.

I finished my pasta and eyed the serving bowl. Gina must have noticed. She'd make a great mom someday—she had a mother's sixth sense.

"Tiramisu," she said. "In the fridge."

"Right."

I put down my fork and picked up my wine, sitting back and looking out at the now-blue horizon and the first couple of stars. Lights sprinkled the hills in the foreground.

We sat chatting and watching the night fall for a while, then cleared the table. In the living room, Gina fired up her movie-streaming gizmo. On the wall between two sets of shelves was a gigantic flat-screen TV.

"Wow, when did you get that?"

She pointed a remote control at the screen and pressed a button, causing the screen to glow blue. "Couple weeks ago. What do you want to see?"

"I don't know. Something lighthearted."

"How about the latest Sandler comedy?"

"Let's give it a whirl."

I joined her on her black leather couch and she pushed buttons until the movie came on. About ten minutes into the film I looked at her.

"Can we make some popcorn?"

"There's tiramisu."

"Not to eat, to throw at the screen."

Gina chortled. "You, too?"

"It's a Big Lie story. I hate those."

"Hey, you approved it!"

"Yeah, and now I'm sorry."

Gina picked up the remote and paused the movie. "OK, so we lose it. Something else you want to see?"

"Yeah. *Charade*. Ever seen it?"

"Nope."

"Can you get it?"

"Let's find out."

More button-pushing. I got up to use the bathroom. Before I could get back to the couch, my cell phone rang from the kitchen.

"Sorry, I forgot to turn it off!"

I hurried to the phone nook and dug the cell out of my purse. The number on the caller ID looked familiar, though it said "Unavailable." I flipped it open.

"Hello?"

"Hi, Ellen, it's Tony. Got some news and I wanted to tell you before you heard it from someone else. The M.E. figured out what killed Mrs. Garcia. It wasn't Whoever's Syndrome."

"Oh? What, then?"

"It was botulism."

9

"Botulism?!"

"Hang on, don't freak out," Tony said. "Are you listening?"

I was breathing fast, and my gut had clenched with panic at the thought that I'd killed one of my customers. I had to concentrate to keep from dropping the phone. I closed my eyes.

"Yes, I'm listening."

"OK, I want you to think about it for a minute. Botulism takes hours to build up to fatal levels in the bloodstream. Days, even."

I took a couple more breaths. My brain seemed to have shut off.

"So she can't have picked it up at the tearoom, right?" Tony said. "She died shortly after she arrived."

"Oh." A cold flood of relief washed through me. "Yes, I see."

"They're testing the food anyway, just to eliminate it as a possible source."

"OK."

"You all right?"

I took a shaky breath. "Uh—yeah. Thanks. Thanks for calling me."

"I figured you'd panic if you heard it in passing."

I gave a nervous laugh. "Yeah."

"It's not your fault, OK? You didn't cause this."

"Right. Thanks."

A pause followed, during which I was able to collect my wits. I was deeply grateful to Tony for going out of his way to call me.

"Sorry I had to run out on you earlier," he said.

"It's OK."

"Any chance you're not busy tomorrow evening? I'd like to make it up to you."

"Oh...no. I mean, yes. I—I don't have any plans."

"How about dinner?"

My stomach clenched again, but for a different reason. "Sounds great," I said.

"You close at six, right? I can pick you up at, say, seven-thirty?"

"Fine."

"See you then."

"Hey, Tony—"

"Yeah?"

"Um, thanks a lot for calling me. I'm grateful."

"No problem. See you tomorrow night."

He hung up. I stood there for a moment, still sorting through all the different feelings of the last couple of minutes.

"Bye," I said softly, though he was long gone.

I turned off the phone and returned to the living room. Gina gave me a curious look.

"Botulism?"

I glanced at her sharply. She shrugged.

"You yelled it. I wasn't eavesdropping."

I took a long breath. "Yeah, botulism. That's what killed Mrs. Garcia, but it didn't come from the tearoom. She had to have gotten it earlier."

Gina frowned. "She didn't put honey in her tea, did she? I know you're not supposed to give honey to babies 'cause they might get botulism. Maybe old ladies are susceptible, too."

I endured a painful moment of trying to recall how Mrs. Garcia had taken her tea before remembering Tony's reassurance. "It can't have been anything at the tearoom. It takes a long time to build up in the bloodstream, and she was there for less than an hour, poor thing."

Gina nodded. "Poor thing indeed. Poor you, too."

"It could have been much worse."

"Yeah, the Bird Woman could have been there."

I tried unsuccessfully to hide a smile of laughter. "Actually, she was."

"No! Was she horrible?"

"Only moderately. At least the press didn't show up."

I went back to the sofa. The TV now displayed a frozen frame from the opening credits of *Charade*. Gina topped off our wineglasses, and I sat back and let myself get immersed in the movie. Compared to Audrey Hepburn's adventures, my life was positively dull.

By the time the film ended I was yawning my head off, despite its exciting conclusion. Long, emotional day and I was exhausted. Gina sent me home with hugs, kisses, and a large chunk of tiramisu which I shamefully intended to eat for breakfast.

I drove home slowly, though by now the alcohol was pretty much out of my system. Warm summer evening and Santa Fe was hopping, more with local kids than with tourists at this point. They liked to cruise, and when the cops cracked down on them for cruising one street they simply moved to another.

I turned onto Marcy Street and passed a candy-apple green low-rider with its speakers booming so loud they throbbed in my gut. The car was stuffed full of Hispanic teenagers and one lone blonde girl. I smiled to myself as the boom faded behind me, remembering my own not-so-distant days of hanging out.

As I turned into the alley that ran behind the tearoom I glimpsed movement among the lilac bushes at the side of the house. I slowed, and considered driving past, but decided that would serve no purpose. It might have been a dog, but if it was a person, driving past would just give him a chance to get away.

I checked to make sure my doors were locked, then shut off my headlights and eased into my usual parking place. I sat for a minute, watching the lilac bushes, keeping an eye on my mirrors, alert to any movement. It was dark, and after a moment I realized the dining parlor lights were off.

Break-in? Or just Captain Dusenberry playing games with me?

I fought down an urge to call Tony. He wasn't my private security service, and I didn't want him to think I was a wimp. I didn't know anything was going on, I just had a feeling.

I took a flashlight out of the glove compartment, aimed it at the lilac bushes, and turned it on. Two dark shapes crouching there jumped and ran, heading toward the street out front.

I got out of the car and hurried after them, trying to get a better look. Heard giggling and caught a glimpse as they turned up the street and disappeared beyond the neighboring building. Kids, dressed in black, a boy and a girl—and the girl's striped stockings looked Goth.

I put the flashlight back in the glove box and collected my purse and my tiramisu. Fumbled at the back door with my keys, then the dining parlor chandelier came on, flooding the *portal* with soft light.

"Oh! Um, thanks," I said, unlocking the door and stepping in.

I was talking to a ghost.

I locked the door behind me and stood for a minute, just listening to the house. It was quiet, calm. On impulse I opened the door to the dining parlor.

The room was in order, the table covered with a fresh lace cloth and a teapot filled with roses in the center, ready to be set in the morning. I glanced up at the chandelier. One crystal was swinging gently back and forth.

I remembered the chandelier blinking earlier. Right before

Rosa had come crying down the hall.

I pulled the door closed.

It was weird, sharing the house with a ghost. Hard to talk about. If I mentioned Captain Dusenberry, even just trying to be funny, people gave me odd looks. There were a few who didn't, but as I thought most of them were nuts, they weren't much comfort.

I went upstairs and crashed. In the morning I rose early, took a long, hot shower, dressed and carried my tiramisu downstairs.

Salsa music greeted me from the kitchen. Julio was already hard at work. He had three trays of round, meringue wafers on the work table and was piping lemon mousse onto one set of them.

"Morning," I said. "Can you take a break?"

Julio glanced up at me, wary. "What for?"

"Tiramisu. I'll trade you some for a cup of coffee."

"Where's it from?"

"My friend Gina made it."

"OK. Let me finish this tray."

I went to the break table in the far corner of the kitchen while he finished making meringue-mousse sandwiches. The table sits by the kitchen's original fireplace, which I seldom use. Usually it's quite warm enough in there, even in winter.

The fireplace is picturesque, though, and I like it. Larger than the fireplaces in the parlors, because it was originally used for cooking. I'd found a couple of antique cooking tools to hang from the old hooks underneath the mantel, and an old cupboard where the staff could stash their belongings.

I got out plates and forks and divided the tiramisu. Julio joined me with two cups of steaming coffee and a carton of cream. I put a splash in my coffee and sipped.

"Mmm. Thank you. You make the best coffee."

Julio nodded, a simple acknowledgment of the truth. He's

got an ego, like any chef, but he doesn't need constant praise. He has confidence in his work. Knowing that, I felt I should do him the same courtesy Tony had done me; tell him about the botulism before he heard it by chance and misunderstood.

"How are you doing?" I said.

"OK. I visited my mom last night."

I winced inside. He must have told her about Maria's death.

"Julio, there's something you should know. They've figured out what killed your grandmother. It was botulism, but she couldn't have been exposed to it here."

Julio sat up straight, bristling. "Damn right she couldn't!"

"Easy. I'm just telling you so you won't be caught off guard."

"Sorry." He picked up his cup. "So where did she get it?"

"I don't know. It might be hard to figure out, unless someone else comes down with it."

For the first time I wondered if any of the rest of Rosa's family was in danger. I resolved to call and check on her later in the morning.

Julio ate a bite of tiramisu, then nodded. "Good. You're friend's a good cook."

I smiled. "She is."

"She looking for work? I could use an assistant."

"Uh—no, she's got a career in advertising. Are you getting overloaded?"

He shrugged. "I'm not complaining."

"When did you get here this morning?"

"Four."

And he usually stayed well past noon. I stifled a sigh. With business increasing, I'd have to hire an assistant for him. I didn't want to risk him burning out and quitting.

"Would a part-timer help?" I asked.

"Anything." He finished his coffee and stood up, leaving his unfinished dessert-breakfast. "I better get back to work.

Thanks for the tiramisu."

"You're welcome."

I finished my own coffee, then covered Julio's leftover tiramisu and put it on the staff shelf in the refrigerator. It was still early, so I grabbed an apron and helped Julio out for an hour or so, happily avoiding the less pleasant task of struggling with the schedule that awaited me up in my office.

Kris came in at nine, recalling me to my sense of administrative duty. I relinquished my apron and made a pot of tea to take upstairs. I was just carrying it out of the pantry when I met Rosa in the hallway, wearing her wisteria server's dress and apron.

"Rosa! I gave you the day off, dear."

"I know, but I'd rather work, if it's OK." She gave a forlorn smile. "Keep my mind off things."

My heart went out to her. If I hadn't had my hands full of tea, I'd have hugged her.

"Of course it is. Actually, I'm very glad you came in. Julio's a bit swamped. Do you think you could help him out until we open?"

"Sure."

Her smile brightened a little, and she turned toward the kitchen. She looked perfectly well, so my fear that she might have been exposed to the botulism was soothed, though I thought I'd better talk to her about it anyway.

"Hang on a second, Rosa." I stepped back into the pantry, gestured to her to follow me, and set the tea tray down. "The police have figured out what caused your grandmother's death, and it's a little unusual."

"It wasn't a stroke?"

"No, dear. I'm afraid it was botulism."

Rosa looked alarmed. "Botulism? Food poisoning?"

"She didn't get it here."

I worried that she was going to cry, but she pulled herself

together when I explained that the tearoom could not possibly be the source of the botulism. That implied, of course, that Maria might have been poisoned by something she ate at home, but I left that for Rosa to figure out on her own. At least now she'd been alerted.

I wanted to send her home, but I knew very well how important it can be to be around people, doing normal things, when one is grieving. Oddly, it can be just as important to be away from people, doing and thinking about nothing. Grief changes, day to day. Rosa had said she wanted normalcy, though, so I respected that. I sent her off to help Julio, took my tea tray upstairs, and poured tea for myself and Kris.

We spent the next half hour trying to figure out how to squeeze a part-time cook into the budget. Unless sales jumped a lot in the next couple of months it would mean operating at a loss. I saw my future income receding into the distance.

"Well, we've got to do it," I said. "I won't risk losing Julio. Go ahead and place an ad."

"I'll put a notice on the website first. Doesn't cost anything. I'll write a draft and run it by you."

"All right." I stood up and picked up my teacup. "By the way, I saw a couple of kids poking around in the side garden last night—looked like they might be Goths."

Kris shot me a hard look. "I'm not the keeper of all Goths in Santa Fe."

"I know you're not. I just thought you might have heard something, if there's a rumor going around about Captain Dusenberry or something like that. Aren't there games that some of you play?"

"Not *my* circle!"

"Sorry! No offense intended."

She hunched a shoulder. "Some of the younger kids like to fool around. Maybe they heard about the ghost, and came looking for him."

"So the community knows about Captain Dusenberry?"

"Yeah. I've been asked about him a few times. You never said he was a secret."

"No, that's true."

I sometimes wished he was a secret, but that definitely wasn't the case. With the tearoom a regular stop on Willow Lane's ghost tour, it was pretty much the opposite.

"All right, Kris, thanks. Would you like more tea?"

"Not yet."

I retreated to my office, dealt with a few tasks there, then went downstairs to get ready for opening. Iz, another of my servers—a shy, quiet girl from Tesuque pueblo—had arrived and was putting out place settings according to the reservation chart Kris had printed the night before. I helped her finish and made a quick check of both parlors to make sure the flowers were all fresh before opening the door to the first waiting customers.

Saturday was our busiest day, booked solid from opening to closing. With Rosa back, things weren't quite as hectic as the previous day, but I was still plenty busy. Before I knew it, the afternoon was half gone.

I was ringing up a customer's purchase in the gift shop when Tony walked in. He met my surprised glance and nodded, then busied himself looking at the china, leaning forward to peer at it with his hands clasped behind his back as if he was afraid to actually touch it.

I finished with the customer and saw her out, then glanced at my watch. "You're a little early."

Tony strolled over to the register. "Official visit, I'm afraid. Can we talk?"

He nodded toward the upper floor. I felt a pang of dread. Had the botulism been in our food after all? My rose petal jam?

I led Tony up to my office and offered him tea or coffee. He declined both, and sat across from me in one of the guest chairs, leaning forward with his elbows on his knees.

"Heard from the M.E. this morning. Final diagnosis is wound botulism."

"Wound botulism? I've never heard of that!"

"It's rare. Very odd for a nice old Hispanic lady to pick it up. M.E. says they see it mostly in druggies—people who use black tar heroin from Mexico—the spores can get in the stuff apparently. Anyway, that's kicked it over to a suspicious death, so guess who's investigating."

My heart sank. "Oh. I see."

Tony took out his pocket notebook and flipped it open. "So if you don't mind, I'll borrow your office. I need to talk to Rosa Garcia."

10

My first instinct was to defend poor Rosa. "You can't suspect her! If you had seen how upset she was—"

"She's not being accused of anything."

"Yet," I said, with rather more edge to my voice than I'd intended.

Tony gave me a look of suppressed impatience. "Look, I don't tell you how to make tea."

"All right." I stood up. "Yes, of course you may use the office. I'll bring Rosa up."

"Thanks."

Remembering Tony's interview technique, I paused in the doorway. "Would you mind if I stayed with her?"

"Frankly, yes."

"I won't say anything, I promise. I just want to lend her moral support. She's young, and she just lost her grandmother."

"Which is why I'm here."

I gave him my best Miss Manners repressive glare. He looked up at the sloping ceiling and heaved a sigh.

"OK. But you say one word and," he gestured toward the door with a thumb.

I smiled. "Promise," I said, and hurried downstairs to collect Rosa.

She was in the pantry dressing trays for the next batch of customers. Julio was gone, and Kris only works half-days on Saturdays, so she had left as well. I ran Iz down in the gift shop and warned her she'd be on her own for a little while.

"No problem, Boss!" she said, then covered her mouth. "I

mean, Ellen."

I gave her a tolerant smile. "We'll be back down as soon as we can."

Returning to the pantry, I found Rosa with her hands full of a pan of hot scones. I helped her add them to the tea trays, then took her upstairs, pausing on the landing to inform her that Tony was here and wanted to talk to her.

"He's been asked to investigate your grandmother's death," I said in a low voice.

"Investigate?" She looked alarmed.

"He just wants to ask you a few questions. I'll stay with you, all right?"

I saw her swallow. "OK."

I led her into the office, where Tony had made himself at home behind my desk. "Rosa, this is Detective Aragón."

She nodded, looking terrified. Tony smiled.

"Hi, Rosa," he said. "Have a seat."

She sat down, and I took the other guest chair. Tony flipped through the pages of his notebook for a moment, then looked up at Rosa.

"Your grandmother lived at Casa de Sónset. How often did you visit her there?"

Rosa blinked. "Once or twice a month, I guess."

"When was the last time you were there?"

"Um." She frowned in thought. "I think it was Mother's Day."

Tony made a note. "Did your father go over there more often?"

"Well, yes."

Rosa cast a nervous glance at me. I smiled to reassure her.

"How often?"

"He's there a couple of times a week, usually. He brings her groceries, fixes things for her."

"And they got along OK?"

"Yes."

"Even though she was technically his employer? Did they ever argue about how he handled the restaurant?"

"Maybe they disagreed a little sometimes. I've never heard them argue."

Tony wrote something in the notebook, then peered at it for a long while. The silence stretched. Rosa fidgeted in her chair.

"How about your mother? She get along OK with your grandmother?"

"Yes."

"Everyone else in the family get along with her?"

Rosa was silent. I saw a frown tighten her brow.

"Mostly," she said finally.

"Mostly?"

Tony stared at her, the flat cop stare that I so dislike. It annoyed me to see him using it on Rosa, but I held my tongue. He glanced at me, then spoke in a gentler tone.

"Who would you say got along with her the least?"

"M-my Aunt Estella. They haven't spoken for years."

"Why?"

Rosa looked down at her hands, and I noticed they were clenched in her lap. "Aunt Estella got a divorce. Nana never forgave her."

"Ah." Tony wrote for a minute, then looked up. "Anyone else?"

"I t-think she was OK with everyone else."

"You think? But you're not sure?"

I frowned at Tony. He was starting to bully. He didn't look at me, but I knew he knew I disapproved.

"Well, Uncle Matt has an Anglo girlfriend, and Nana didn't like that." Rosa turned her head to look at me. "Sorry."

I smiled, letting her know I understood. Mrs. Garcia had been conservative about her family, I gathered. Not that unusual.

In New Mexico, Hispanics and Anglos share a lot of things —political power, economic power, cultural influence—but there are sometimes invisible lines that one crosses at one's own risk. A powerful woman like Mrs. Garcia would be able to draw such lines for those under her influence.

Tony bent to his notepad. "What's the girlfriend's name?"

"Sherry, uh—Anderson, I think."

"What's she like?"

Rosa shrugged. "I've only met her a couple of times. Uncle Matt doesn't bring her to a lot of family parties. She's nice, I guess."

"How long have they been dating?"

"Um, maybe five, six years?"

Tony gazed at her thoughtfully. "Are they living together?"

A faint blush came into Rosa's cheeks. She nodded. "For about a year. Nana didn't approve."

Tony made another note. I kept a concerned eye on Rosa. She was bearing up all right, but she didn't look comfortable. I glanced at my watch, debating whether to put a stop to it by saying we had to get back to work.

"What about you?" Tony asked. "How did you get along with your grandmother?"

Rosa broke into a beaming smile. "She was the best! She was my champion."

"Your champion?"

Rosa nodded. "When I wanted to come work here, and Papa didn't want me to, she said to let me make my own choices." Rosa looked at me. "She said if I could succeed in the Anglo world, all the better for me."

Tony caught my eye and looked smug. I chose to ignore it. He leaned back in my chair and looked down at his notes.

"You know of anyone who might've been mad at your grandmother?"

Rosa gazed at him, looking bewildered, then shook her

head. "No. She's strict, but everyone loves her. Even Aunt Estella."

"What about someone outside the family?"

Rosa shrugged. "The other restaurant managers, maybe. I don't know. I haven't heard anything."

"OK. Thanks."

Tony sat frowning at his notes for a long moment. Rosa shifted in her chair.

"Is that it? Can I go?"

Tony glanced up at her. "Yeah, you can go."

Rosa stood up at once, looking relieved. I followed her to the door, but paused there and waited until she had gone downstairs, then looked back at Tony.

"I hope you got what you needed."

Tony glanced at me. "Oh, yeah. Big help. Hadn't heard about the Anglo girlfriend. Course I haven't talked to Matt yet, but it's interesting that Ricardo didn't mention it."

"Families protect their secrets."

"And matriarchs rule with a rod of iron." Tony stood up and came to the door, stuffing his notebook in a pocket. "Maybe Uncle Matt and his girlfriend will have an easier time of it now."

"You're not suggesting—"

"Nope. Not suggesting anything. Just cogitating. Hell, I don't even know if we have a crime here. She could have picked it up accidentally. Botulism exists pretty commonly in plain old dirt, the M.E. told me."

"She was a gardener," I said, thinking of our brief conversation about roses.

"Yeah? So maybe she got a cut dirty. Could just be bad luck."

"In that case, why are you interviewing her family?"

"Hey, it's job security. I'm told to investigate, I investigate. Speaking of which, I need to talk to the grandson." He consulted his notebook. "Julio Delgado."

"He's gone home for the day. He comes in early."

"OK, I'll catch him later." He stepped past me into the upper hall. "Thanks for the use of your office."

"You're welcome."

"See you in a couple of hours."

His eyelids drooped a little as he said that, very sexy. My pulse increased a bit.

"What should I wear?"

He shrugged. "You always look great."

"I was thinking along the lines of motorcycle or not."

"Oh. Not." He grinned. "See you."

He took the stairs at a run, though he didn't make too much noise. I, being in Proprietress mode, made a more dignified descent, arriving at the ground floor just in time to see Tony holding the front door for three elderly women. I smiled and went to greet them as Tony headed out.

"Good afternoon. Do you have a reservation?"

The tallest, who looked smart in a pink linen suit and matching hat, said, "Timothy. Joan."

I stepped to the podium and checked the reservation list. "Ah, yes. You're in Jonquil. Right this way."

The ladies made admiring noises as I led them through the parlor to their seating area. A breeze was disturbing the lace curtains in Jonquil and I lowered the window, leaving it open just a crack.

"This is lovely," said Ms. Timothy. She waved a hand, taking in the whole parlor. "Tell me, do you ever open up this room for larger functions?"

"We can, yes. We also have a dining parlor that seats up to twelve."

She exchanged a glance with one of the other ladies, who shrugged. One of them, whose dress was a floral print with a white, lace-edged collar, said, "That would work for a board meeting, but not for the whole group."

"Are you planning an event?" I asked.

Ms. Timothy smiled. "We have an annual dinner, and we thought we'd do something a little different this year. Perhaps a tea."

"Everyone expects a dinner," said the third woman, who wore a simple dress of green cotton and looked a trifle grumpy.

"And I do think this place is a little small," said the woman in the floral dress in a worried tone. She glanced at me. "No offense, but it's fifty people or so, usually, at the dinner."

I nodded. "I understand, though we had close to seventy at our grand opening. That was more of a reception, with a full afternoon tea. We used this room and had overflow into the smaller parlor and the dining parlor. Now that the weather's warmer we could also overflow out onto the *portal*."

"Hmm. That might work." Ms. Timothy looked out the window at the wisteria-shaded *portal*. "The setting is certainly perfect. You have beautiful roses. Do you do your own gardening?"

"Yes, I do. Thank you."

"You should consider joining the Rose Guild," said the worried woman, smiling at me as if to make up for her doubts about having an event here.

"You're the second person this week to suggest that to me," I said.

"Really?" said Ms. Timothy. "Who was the first?"

Too late, I realized the awkwardness of bringing up Mrs. Garcia. I held onto my smile, reflecting that I didn't have to mention the circumstances of her advising me to join the Rose Guild. I caught sight of Iz by the flower urn, waiting to bring in a tray with a cozy-covered teapot.

"It was Maria Garcia," I said pleasantly, and was about to step out of Iz's way, but I stopped when I saw their reactions.

Ms. Timothy looked aghast. Ms. Grumpy looked smug, and Ms. Worried looked viciously angry.

11

"Oh, poor dear Maria!" said Ms. Timothy. "We just heard about her unfortunate demise. That's one of the things we're going to talk about today, what to do for her memorial."

She glanced at the other ladies. Ms. Worried had controlled her features, but still looked annoyed.

"I don't see the need to do anything at all," she said.

"Lucy!"

"You know all she did was cause trouble!"

Ms. Grumpy joined the fray. "That's not entirely true."

Lucy looked at her in surprise. The moment had become awkward, and I couldn't think what to say, being preoccupied with wondering if these ladies knew how close they were standing to where Maria Garcia had died.

Iz came to the rescue. "Here's your tea, ladies," she said, stepping in as if the outburst hadn't happened.

Recalled to their situation, the ladies settled themselves in the comfortable wing chairs grouped around the low table. Iz poured tea for them while I shamefully beat a retreat to the pantry. I was curious about their apparent familiarity with Mrs. Garcia, but the conversation had disintegrated so disastrously that the only thing to do was pretend it hadn't happened and start afresh.

Rosa was setting up two food trays, one for the party in Jonquil and one for our last reservation of the day, a party of four who hadn't arrived yet. A pot of tea for them was already steeping. I helped arrange the savories and sweets on the trays.

"You look a little tired, Rosa. Would you like to go home? Iz and I can handle things until closing."

She gave me a grateful look. "If you don't mind. I've sort of got a headache."

Poor thing. The interview with Tony had rattled her. I squeezed her shoulder.

"Go on home, then. Get some rest."

She untied the strings of her apron. "Thanks, Ellen. See you on Tuesday. Oh...or Monday. That's when the memorial service is."

"Well, then I'll see you there," I said gently.

She nodded and made a game attempt to smile, though I could see tears gleaming in her eyes. She hung up her apron and ducked into the kitchen to fetch her purse from the staff cupboard. A moment later she called a quiet goodbye as she left by the back door.

Iz came into the pantry. "Lily's here. I just seated them."

"Good, there's their tea. I sent Rosa home, so it's just you and me."

Iz glanced at the trays. "I should check on Iris."

"Go ahead, I'll get the scones."

She took the infuser out of Lily's teapot and covered it with a cozy, then carried it away. I went into the kitchen to fetch the day's last pan of scones from the oven.

They smelled fantastic, and I had the urge to gobble one of the extras, but I didn't want to spoil my dinner with Tony. I arranged scones on the center plates of the tiered food trays, set dishes of fresh lemon curd and clotted cream alongside them, then reached for the bowl of rose petals to decorate the trays.

Roses. Rose Guild. I wondered if the organization the ladies in Jonquil belonged to was the Guild. They knew Maria Garcia, and she'd been a member. Their reaction to her name made me curious about Maria's participation in the Guild. They must at least have some regard for her if they were planning a memorial.

I picked out the best petals and scattered them over the ladies' tray, then carried it up to the front parlor. "Here you are, ladies," I said as I set the tray in the center of their table.

"Thank you," said Ms. Timothy. "Oh, rose petals! How pretty!"

"You mentioned the Rose Guild," I said. "Are you members?"

"Yes, we're the officers of the Guild. I'm the President, Lucy Kingston here is Secretary Treasurer—" she gestured to Ms. Worried, then to Ms. Grumpy, "—and Cora Young is our Vice President."

"manila," muttered Ms. Young.

I nodded and smiled at each of them in turn. "I'm delighted to meet you. I'm Ellen Rosings. I would love to learn more about your group."

Ms. Timothy gestured toward the fourth chair. "Won't you join us?"

"Thank you. I need to see to a couple of things. Perhaps in a few minutes."

I handed them each a menu card, leaving them to fend for themselves at figuring out which items were what, and went to check on the other parties. Iris wanted another pot of tea, so I started it brewing.

The day was winding down. Iz was manning the register as departing parties browsed in the gift shop. I stopped into the kitchen, where Mick was conquering the day's heap of dirty dishes. I took Iris their tea, then went to sit with the ladies from the Rose Guild, who had worked their way through their savories and were now starting on the scones.

"Well, we should definitely send some roses to the service at the very least," Ms. Timothy was saying as I walked in. "Oh, hello, Miss Rosings!"

"Please call me Ellen," I said, stepping to the vacant chair.

"Thank you, and please call me Joan." She smiled at me, then glanced at the other ladies. "I was just saying we should send roses to Maria's memorial service. Do you happen to know when it is?"

"Monday, I believe. I don't know the details."

"Well, it'll be in the paper." She picked up her teacup and sighed. "Such a sad thing. She had just come back from an injury."

I nodded. The other two ladies said nothing. Lucy Kingston looked airily out of the window as she sipped her tea, and Cora Young was occupied in spreading lemon curd on a scone.

"How well did you know her, Ellen?" asked Joan.

"Not well at all. We only recently met, but her granddaughter works here."

"Oh. So you must have heard all about it."

"How did she die?" asked Ms. Kingston, leaning toward me with a hint of suppressed eagerness that reminded me forcibly of the Bird Woman.

"I don't want to spoil your tea by talking about it," I said gently.

"My dear, it would take more than Maria Garcia to spoil my appetite!"

I glanced at Joan, who gave a small, sympathetic shrug. "Go ahead and tell us, if you don't mind."

"Well, I understand the cause of death was wound botulism."

"Oh, dear! She must have picked it up gardening," said Joan. "I never could convince her to wear gloves. She said she liked to feel the earth with her hands."

"Stubborn," said Ms. Kingston, reaching for a scone.

Ms. Young nodded in agreement. An awkward silence fell, which Joan broke by clearing her throat.

"Well, we must send flowers for the service, and I think we should place a memorial bench in the City Rose Garden as well."

"If we placed a bench for every member who died, there wouldn't be room to walk in the garden," said Ms. Kingston.

"But Maria has been a member for over twenty years," Joan said, "and she was Vice President for the past five. And I believe she left a bequest to the Guild. She told me she intended to. A permanent memorial is the least we owe her."

I couldn't help wondering what the amount of the bequest might have been. Enough that someone would kill for it?

Silently reprimanding myself, I returned my attention to the Rose Guild ladies as they shifted their discussion to their annual dinner. Joan was enthusiastic about making it a tea reception at the Wisteria Tearoom, and having sampled Julio's wonderful food, the other ladies seemed more willing to discuss it now.

"I can have my chef draw up a menu, if you like," I offered. "No need to decide right away."

"Yes, please do," said Joan. "And why don't we reserve a date, just in case? We've been looking at the 28th."

We discussed a few more details, and I fetched three copies of Kris's excellent brochure for the ladies to take away. Joan gave me a Rose Guild card in exchange and thanked me warmly. I escorted them all out, and gratefully locked the front door behind them.

Glancing at my watch, I saw that it was almost half past six. I had an hour to finish up downstairs and change for my date.

Date. The word made my insides quail. I hadn't really gone out on a date since before my parents had died.

I distracted myself with helping Iz and Mick shut the tearoom down for the weekend. Sundays and Mondays we were closed, and I was looking forward more than usual to the time off.

At ten to seven I waved goodbye to Iz and Mick from the back door and hurried upstairs to get ready. Stripping off my

Victorian dress, I hunted through my wardrobe for something less lacy.

Most of my dresses were for the tearoom, but I had a few others: a sober navy day dress, which I'd be needing on Monday; a couple of cocktail dresses; a couple of sun dresses; and a clingy, full-skirted dress of deep violet that was fun for dancing. It wasn't the sexiest dress I owned—that was probably the black strapless cocktail dress—but it was sexy enough. I didn't want Tony to think I was desperate, after all.

I showered and dressed, and decided to wear my hair down, just caught back in a purple velvet hairband that matched my dress. I cast an anxious glance in my bedroom mirror, tugged at the dress to straighten it, and wondered if I should wear the cocktail dress after all.

"No, that way lies madness."

I stepped firmly away from the mirror and picked up my purse. I was ready with five minutes to spare, so I went downstairs and out onto the front *portal* to watch for Tony.

Evening sunlight was slanting in from the west. I pulled a wicker chair into the shade of one of the wisteria vines and sat enjoying the chance to relax. A slight breeze stirred the leaves and brought the scent of roses up onto the *portal*.

I had plans for serving out here, eventually, but I would need to build up to it. More tables and chairs, more linens and china, and more staff would be necessary, and right now I just couldn't swing it. Maybe next year.

I mused about the Rose Guild's event. I could rent extra furniture for that. Five or six small tables would probably fit on the *portal*. The Guild's reception would be the largest event I had ever hosted, not counting my opening reception, if they did decide to have it here.

My thoughts were interrupted by the sound of a motorcycle. I glanced up, then remembered Tony had said we wouldn't be riding. I hoped he hadn't changed his mind, because the violet dress was not at all suited for a bike.

The motorcycle was a hot red number ridden by a *cholo* kid with a headband. No helmet of course. Shades and a muscle shirt. He roared on up the street and I watched him out of sight, wondering if Tony had been like that when he was younger.

The "chunk" of a car door drew my attention to the front gate, and I saw Tony standing by a dark green sedan parked at the curb. I jumped up, then made myself take a long breath and let it out before strolling down the path to the gate.

Tony watched me, grinning. His eyes were hidden by his usual cop shades, but nothing else was usual. He wore a long-sleeved burgundy shirt that looked like silk, with just a slight flare above the cuffs, and an actual necktie of dark silver brocade. Gray slacks, a matching coat lying on the back seat of the sedan, and polished black shoes. He looked classy.

"Hey, gorgeous," he said, opening the gate for me, and my heart jittered in my chest.

"I bet you say that to all the tearoom owners," I said to hide my nervousness.

Tony opened the sedan's passenger door. "All the gorgeous ones."

I slid into the seat and collected my skirt. Tony closed the door, then went around and jumped into the driver's seat.

"Nice car."

"It's my mother's."

"Oh. Nice of her to lend it to you."

"Yeah."

"You don't sound very enthusiastic."

He looked across at me and grimaced slightly. "It talks."

I chuckled. "You can turn that off, I think."

"My mom likes it." He put the key in the ignition and started the engine.

"Please fasten your seat belt," said the car.

"Oh!" I said. "Sorry."

I hastily buckled my belt. Tony grimaced again, and pulled into traffic.

He drove around to the south side of downtown, then turned onto the Old Santa Fe Trail. Southeast, heading out of town, away from most of the restaurants, but there were a few out that way. I didn't try to guess where he was taking me. It was nice just to enjoy the ride and the evening.

Outside of town Tony pulled into the lot of the Steaksmith, a restaurant that had once been in town but had moved to the outskirts of Santa Fe decades ago. He parked and helped me out of the car as the sun was starting to set. I looked around at the piñon-studded hillsides and smiled.

"I haven't been here in ages."

"It's still good," Tony said, shrugging into his jacket.

"Glad to hear it." I smiled and slid my hand into the elbow he offered, and strolled with him up to the door.

The maître d' whisked us to a table in the front dining room. Tony accepted the wine list without hesitation and chose a bottle of very nice cabernet. We both ordered steaks, and I asked for a side of sauteed mushrooms, a dish I remembered fondly. The waiter brought wine and water and tactfully disappeared.

"So," Tony said, picking up his glass. "Here's to the real weekend."

I smiled and met the toast, then tasted the wine. "Good choice."

"Thanks."

"I didn't know you knew wines."

"I've picked up a little here and there. I'm no expert."

"No one's a complete expert."

He smiled. Without the shades the tough cop look was gone. I was curious whether he'd interviewed any more of the Garcia family, but it was so nice to see him looking relaxed that I didn't want to remind him of work.

"So, your mom drives a talking car. What else does she do?"

"She's a hairdresser. Works at a salon at one of the malls."

"Oh. I wondered if maybe she was retired."

"Not yet."

What I was really wondering was why Tony didn't own his own car. I'd suspected it might be because he was supporting a family member, but apparently it wasn't his mother.

I remembered him mentioning that his grandmother lived in an inexpensive (he'd called it crummy) apartment, and that his sister took care of her. Maybe he was subsidizing the grandmother.

I sipped my wine. "You have a sister, right? Any other siblings?"

"Two sisters. One's married, the other's in college. Older brother in the army."

"Ah."

College could cost a bundle, probably more than a hairdresser could afford. I was willing to bet that Tony was putting his sister through school, and supporting his grandmother.

"How about you?" he asked after a minute.

"I have a brother. He lives in New York."

"That's it?"

"Well, you've met my Aunt Natasha. My parents are dead."

I don't know why I said that so abruptly. Tony probably already knew it, but I couldn't remember if we'd talked about my folks.

"Sounds kind of lonely," he said.

I shrugged. "Sometimes. I have friends, though. And the tearoom keeps me busy."

"Going okay so far, is it?"

"So far, yes. I could stand not to have any more customers

dying in the place."

Tony guffawed, and I chuckled too. It was ridiculous, after all. I'd been open for two months, and had two ladies fetch up dead in that time.

Our salads arrived. I said "yes" to fresh ground pepper, and we both sat stock still while the waiter wielded a yard-long pepper mill, only relaxing when he went away.

Tony picked up his fork and poked at his salad. "So, would you, um." He cleared his throat. "Would you like to go to a movie some time?"

He wasn't looking at me. Nerves?

"That sounds nice. I don't get to the movies very often these days. I don't even know what's showing."

"I picked up a paper. It's in the car."

"Good thinking," I said, taking note that his movie invitation was premeditated.

"There's one called *Pretty in Mink.*"

"Sounds like a girl movie. Aren't you more an action-adventure kind of guy?"

He shrugged and picked up his wine glass. "I get enough of that at work."

"I thought police work was ninety-nine percent boredom—"

"Yeah, but the one percent sheer terror more than makes up for it."

I watched him stab at his salad. "So that saying is true?"

He glanced up at me. "Pretty much."

"Sorry. I shouldn't have brought it up over dinner."

He mentioned a couple of other movies that were current. I hadn't heard of either of them; the tearoom had been the center of my life for the past year.

We managed to get halfway through our steaks before talking about police work again. Tony glanced up at me as he was cutting a bite of meat.

"I talked to Uncle Matt after I left your place."

"Matt Garcia?"

"Yeah. Seems okay. Upset about his mom dying, but also relieved, and feeling guilty for being relieved. All normal stuff."

"Did you meet the girlfriend?"

"Yeah, I talked to them both at their condo. He's a lawyer. She runs a gallery."

I raised my eyebrows. Money. Big money, probably. Law school was not cheap. Having a rich and powerful matriarch could be a huge advantage for an Hispanic guy trying to get ahead in the world. I wondered for an instant what Tony's life would be like if he'd had one.

"Maria pay for the gallery?" I asked.

"Oh, not even! Maria wouldn't have anything to do with Sherry Anderson. It sounds like she actually hated her."

"That could be very awkward if Uncle Matt owed Mom money."

"He didn't. He insisted on paying her back for putting him through school, even though she didn't want the money. He didn't want to owe her anything, and he makes a good living as a lawyer."

"So he wouldn't have a desperate need for whatever he might inherit," I said.

"Nope. But now he and Sherry can get married."

12

I sat up, surprised. "Are they? Getting married?"

Tony picked up his wineglass. "Yeah. Mama Maria was totally against it, which is the only reason they didn't do it before. Now they can."

I watched him drink, wondering if he'd meant it as a toast. Wondering if he was comparing Matt and Sherry's situation to ours, as I was. What would Tony's family say if he decided to marry a white girl?

"Does the rest of the family support them?" I asked.

He hunched a shoulder. "Some more than others. It doesn't matter. Maria was the authority figure, and now she's gone. Nobody else in the family has power over Matt like she did. And she did, even without the money."

I frowned. "You don't think—"

"I'm just collecting information. I'll do the thinking later."

"I don't believe you. You're always thinking."

He glanced up at me sharply, then broke into a slow grin. "You're right. But I can't talk about my speculations."

Wouldn't talk about them, more like. I ate a mushroom and washed it down with the last of my wine. Tony picked up the bottle and offered to refill my glass.

"Half," I said. "Well, if you can't talk about your speculations, I'll talk about mine. Did you know that Maria Garcia was a member of the Rose Guild?"

Tony topped off his own wine. "I think that's in my notes somewhere."

"I met three of their members today. It sounds to me like Maria made some waves."

Tony looked intrigued. "Politics?"

"That might be too strong a word. Certainly some interesting group dynamics."

"Hm. I'll have to check into it."

"Or I could."

Tony frowned. "No amateur detective stuff, please."

"No, just gossip-mongering. I'm curious. You can't tell me not to follow it up."

"No, I can't, but don't muddy the waters, okay?"

"What waters? It's the Rose Guild. It was a hobby. Even if there were nasty politics going on, I doubt any of them would kill over it."

He nodded. "You're probably right, but I'd still like you to steer clear of them."

"Well, I can't. I'm negotiating to host an event for them."

I drank some more wine. It was making me a little reckless, maybe. I was enjoying teasing Tony.

"By the way," I added, "the Guild's president mentioned that Maria Garcia promised them a bequest."

Tony's frown deepened. "Big one?"

"I haven't the foggiest. You mean you haven't got hold of a copy of her will?"

"Not yet, but I will."

"I'd be curious to know who else got bequests."

"I can tell you that without looking. The church got the biggest chunk, her pet charity the next biggest, and the rest got divvied between family and friends and a few other bequests like this rose club. That's just the cash—the restaurants go to the family."

"According to Matt?"

Tony nodded. "He drew up the will."

"Think he might have slipped something in?"

"No. He's an honorable guy."

I gazed at Tony over my wine. "I like honorable guys," I

said softly.

He gazed back at me, speculation in those Spanish eyes and the slight frown melting into a smile. I smiled back. The wine and the excellent dinner had made me mellow. Mellow and dangerously receptive.

The waiter came to clear our plates and left a dessert menu. Tony glanced at it, then offered it to me.

"Want dessert?"

I shook my head. "I'm around sweets all day. Go ahead if you want something."

"How about just coffee?"

"Sure."

He ordered for us and I sat back, sipping the last of my wine. A waiter had raised the shades on the windows across the room after the sun was down. It was dark outside now. I wondered how late it was, then decided I didn't want to know. I was enjoying the evening and didn't want it to end.

I felt Tony's his gaze on me and turned my head to meet it. Soft, dark eyes.

"When'd you graduate high school?" he asked.

"Oh-five. Why?"

"Who'd you go to prom with?"

"I didn't go to prom."

"Why not?"

I finished my wine and set down the empty glass. "No one asked me."

"Get out of here!"

"It's true. I was one of those introverted, nerdy types."

"Yeah, but..." He shook his head in amazement. "You didn't even get one invitation?"

"Nope. Who'd you go with?"

"Sylvia Montoya."

"She was a cheerleader, wasn't she?"

"Yeah. How'd you know? I thought you went to Santa Fe

High."

I fiddled with my empty wineglass, turning it around by the stem. The conversation was making me slightly uncomfortable.

"Marching band," I said. "Went to a lot of football games."

Tony laughed. "You're kidding me!"

"Nope."

"I don't believe it!"

"I'll show you my yearbook if you insist. Why's it so hard to believe?"

"I just can't picture you in a band uniform."

I laughed. Coffee arrived, and I stirred some cream into mine. When I looked up Tony was watching me with those soft eyes again.

"Why did you ask about prom?" I said.

"I was trying to figure out if I'd ever met you in high school."

"Oh. I don't think so."

"Yeah. I think I would have remembered."

I took a sip of coffee, feeling shy all of a sudden. Maybe it was thinking about high school days, a time of painful vulnerability.

"Did you play football in high school?" I asked.

"Nah. Basketball. And baseball my sophomore year, but I wasn't that great at it."

"Bet you looked great in the uniform, though."

He looked at me, then broke into suppressed laughter. "Better than you in a band uniform!"

"Pig."

I threw a sugar packet at him. He laughed harder.

I tried to frown at him, not very successfully. "That's the last time I'll try to pay you a compliment."

"Oh, I hope not." He subsided, still grinning.

I looked away, pretending to be more offended than I was.

Tony saw right through it, but he humored me. I guess when you're a cop you learn to pick up on people's moods.

We finished our coffee, declined refills, and left after Tony paid the bill. Outside, the night air was delicious—just cool enough to be energizing on top of a big meal. I took a deep breath, savoring the smell of piñon on the summer air, gazing up at the stars.

"Want to go someplace else, or should I take you home?" Tony said.

"Mm." I rubbed my belly. "Too full for dancing."

"We could go somewhere for a drink. I still owe you a margarita."

"No, you owe you a margarita. Mine was just fine, thanks. Oh, damn!" My cell phone was ringing in my purse. "Sorry, I forgot to turn it off."

Tony grinned. "Mine's turned off."

"Well, sorry."

I fished out the phone and looked at the caller ID. It read "SFPD." I frowned.

"That can't be right." I flipped the phone open. "Hello?"

"Hi, Ellen? It's Kris."

"Kris?" I glanced at Tony. "What's up?"

"Um, I'm really sorry to bother you but I was wondering if you could maybe help me out." Her voice sounded nervous. "I don't have anyone else to call. My folks live in Milwaukee, and we're not exactly on friendly terms anyway—"

I felt slightly impatient at the inopportune timing of the call, but Kris had done so much for me that I didn't hesitate. "I'd be happy to help you if I can," I said. "What's the matter? Where are you?"

"I'm down at the city police station. I need you to come bail me out."

13

"Bail you out?! Kris, what happened?" I glanced at Tony but he had walked away a couple of steps and stood looking out at the city lights.

"Um, it's sort of a long story," Kris said. "Don't worry, I didn't do anything horrible. I'll pay you right back, I've got the money."

"How much do you need?"

"Two hundred fifty dollars. They'll want cash."

My heart was beating fast. I pressed a hand to one throbbing temple. "OK. All right. I'll be right there."

"Thanks, Ellen. I'm really sorry about this."

"We'll talk about it when I get there."

"Okay. Bye."

I slid my phone back into my purse. The panic was ebbing, but I still felt anxious to get to Kris as fast as I could. Poor thing, locked up in jail with all the Saturday night drunks and hookers! I had to get her out of there.

"Tony, I'm sorry, but I'm going to have to ask you to take me home."

He turned around, looking apprehensive. "Problem?"

"Yes. My manager's in jail." His expression registered in my brain and I had a sudden awful thought. "You wouldn't happen to know why?"

He winced. "I might have a guess."

My chest filled with anger. "Tony Aragón! This is your doing!"

"No, it isn't, I swear! Honest, all I did was pass a tip on to the Party Patrol."

"Party Patrol? What tip?!"

He hunched up his shoulders. "Um. A tip that there might be an absinthe party in town this weekend."

"Absinthe?!"

"It's popular with the Goths."

"So what? Didn't they legalize it a few years back?"

"Yeah. But those Goths, they like experimenting. Sometimes with drugs."

"I don't believe it! Kris would not mess around with illegal substances."

"Sometimes it's not technically illegal. Designer stuff, just different enough chemically to be considered a different thing. They can be dangerous, though."

I must have looked unimpressed. He ran a hand through his hair.

"Look, we've had some problems with the Goth kids in town lately. They like to throw these absinthe parties—big parties, sometimes with minors involved."

A gust of wind blew my hair across my face. I pushed it back.

"And what made you think there was an absinthe party this weekend?" I demanded.

Tony sighed. "I recognized the shipping label on that box your manager had. It's a company in Europe that sells absinthe. I didn't name names, I swear to God!"

"But the Goth community in Santa Fe can't be that big. Tony, you knew you could get Kris arrested!"

"Well...."

I stared at him, breathing hard. "Take me home. Now."

"Or, um, I could drive you to the station."

I said nothing, just stood glaring. He couldn't have considered what it might be like to have me and Kris in his car under these circumstances.

"You're right," he said after a moment. "I'll take you

home."

He unlocked the car and got in. I pressed my fingers to my eyes before getting in myself. I was so angry I was ready to cry, but I was not going to do it in front of Tony.

I opened the car door.

"The door is ajar," said the car.

I got in and slammed it shut.

"Please fasten your seat belt," said the car.

"Shut up," Tony muttered.

I fastened my belt and locked my door. I couldn't bring myself to look at Tony or to speak to him, so I stared straight ahead with my arms crossed.

He drove sedately back to the tearoom. I fumed the whole way. We didn't speak until he had pulled up at the front gate.

"Look, I'm sorry," Tony said. "I wasn't trying to get your manager in trouble."

"You could have turned a blind eye."

"Not and remained honorable," he said softly.

I looked at him, still angry but I knew he was right. He'd been doing his duty as an officer of the law.

I couldn't deal with my mixed feelings right then. I collected my purse and unbuckled my seat belt.

"Thank you for a lovely evening," I said coldly.

"Please fasten your seat belt," said the car.

"Are you irreconcilably angry with me?" Tony asked.

"At the moment, yes, I am. Ask me again tomorrow." I got out of the car and stood staring at Tony.

"The door is ajar," said the car.

"Shut up!" we both shouted.

Tony looked at me with apologetic eyes. I pushed the door closed with careful restraint, then turned and went through the gate without looking back.

I hurried up the path to the tearoom and let myself in the front door. Didn't turn on a light, just ran up the stairs in the dimness. Didn't listen for the sound of Tony driving away.

At the top of the stairs I paused and took a couple of deep breaths, trying to calm down. My better judgment had begun to look at the situation, and I realized that Tony had actually exercised restraint. Kris had been pretty smart-mouthed with him about her package. Cops didn't take kindly to that.

Some of my anger began to shift to Kris. What the hell had she been thinking? She'd practically dared him to get a warrant! Of course he'd been suspicious!

Soft music began to play through the house speakers downstairs, sending soothing strains of harp floating up to me. Captain Dusenberry—or old wiring—had turned on the stereo.

I closed my eyes briefly, then went into Kris's office and flicked the light switch. The stained glass chandelier cast a pool of warm light onto her desk and a darker, jeweled glow onto her print of Millais's "Ophelia" on the opposite wall.

Repressing an urge to join Ophelia in her watery solace, I went to Kris's desk, wincing as the floor creaked beneath my step. I unlocked the desk drawer and took out the bank bag with the day's receipts from the tearoom. I extracted two hundred fifty dollars, replaced it with a note saying "IOU $250, ER," and locked the bag in the drawer again.

Stuffing the money in my purse, I hurried back downstairs and out the back door. Dining parlor light glowed softly on the *portal*. I jumped into my car and drove to the police station, clenching my teeth and strictly observing the speed limits.

It took over an hour to arrange for a bond. Finally Kris was released to my custody. She came out wearing a black dress of multiple layers of shredded gauze, Queen-of-Sheba makeup that was somewhat smeared, and a look of chagrin.

"Thanks, Ellen. I really appreciate this."

"Yes, well, we'll discuss it elsewhere. Thank you, officer," I said to the desk sergeant.

He handed Kris a lumpy manila envelope with her name scrawled on it in magic marker. Kris peered into it, then meekly followed me out of the station.

I unlocked the car and got in, but before starting the engine I turned to look at Kris. "Do you want me to take you to your car, or do you want to come have a cup of tea and talk about this?"

"It's up to you," she said humbly.

"I think the sooner we sort it out the better we'll both sleep."

"Okay."

I drove back to the tearoom and parked by the back door. The lights were still on and the music still playing.

While Kris made a beeline for the restroom, I went into the butler's pantry and started a pot of Assam tea—warm and toasty, comforting like a mother's hug. I raided the staff shelf in the fridge for leftover cucumber sandwiches, tiny fudge-frosted brownies, and a couple of scones. I warmed the scones in the microwave, carried the food into the dining parlor along with china and accoutrements for two, then fetched the tea from the pantry.

Kris joined me in the dining parlor, having spent the time tidying her appearance. Her hair was combed, and she'd scaled back the makeup to something more like her workday look. The Morticia dress and knee-high lace-up boots couldn't be helped, and I deigned to overlook them. I poured tea for us both.

"You're really angry, aren't you?" Kris asked as I handed her a cup.

I pushed the sugar bowl toward her and poured milk into my own cup. "What makes you think that?"

"You're acting like Miss Manners Supreme," she said, picking up the sugar tongs.

I stirred my tea. "Well, yes. I'm angry. What on earth were

you thinking?"

"I'm sorry. It was supposed to be a private party."

"But it turned out to be more?"

Her face took on a look of frustrated annoyance. "Somebody passed the word around, and a lot of people who weren't originally invited showed up, including some younger kids. Underage."

I held back my bristling temper, strictly controlling my voice. "And yet you stayed? It didn't occur to you to leave a party where minors were consuming alcohol and God knows what else?"

"I...no. I didn't think of that. Ellen, I'm sorry. I'm really sorry!"

She sounded genuinely contrite. My indignation melted. I took a sip of my tea and set the cup down again.

"Apology accepted."

I moved the food plate between us. We both reached for the brownies. Chocolate seemed necessary at the moment.

After consuming a cocoa-based sugar-bomb and washing it down with tea, I was fortified to continue. I warmed up both our cups and picked up a cucumber sandwich.

"Were there illegal substances at that party?"

"I don't know. Like I said, a lot of strangers showed up. The people I hang with aren't into mushrooms or any of that crap."

"Just wormwood. It's poisonous, isn't it?"

Her lips flattened into a line. "Wormwood is. Absinthe isn't."

"I thought it could cause hallucinations."

"That attitude is so nineteenth-century!"

"It isn't attitude," I said quietly. "It's concern."

"Well, it's based on misinformation! Absinthe isn't dangerous if it's made properly. It's just a liqueur."

I examined my sandwich, choosing where to take the first bite. "What exactly were you charged with?"

"Interfering with police."

I looked up at her in surprise.

"They were going after Clarice, who was hosting the party. It wasn't her fault that those kids showed up, so I told them to leave her alone!"

"It's really not a good idea to talk back to police officers."

"Now you sound like my mother!"

The ultimate insult. I winced, then lowered the sandwich.

"I'm just worried, Kris. I don't want to see you in serious trouble."

She glowered. "Or what? Gonna fire me?"

"I hope not. You're an absolute gem, and I'd hate to have to do without you. That's why I'm concerned. That and the fact that I like you."

She glanced away, reached for a scone and chopped it open, then gooped lemon curd onto half of it. I took a bite of my sandwich and watched her eat, hoping she'd simmer down enough to listen to me.

She was only three or four years younger than I. It wasn't as though I couldn't understand her situation.

I felt a wave of loneliness, much as I had frequently felt in high school. I'd always been somewhat out of step, even with my own class. Never mind popularity; I'd had trouble fitting in with the band and orchestra geeks. That awkwardness hit me again now as I watched Kris, who was so grounded in her chosen community.

Not a path I would have chosen myself, but I could see why she had gone Goth. There was a certain temptation to toying with darkness.

"I dyed my hair black, once," I said. "In mid-school."

That made her look up. She stared for a few seconds, then shook her head. "Sorry, I can't picture you in black."

"You're right. It's not a good color for me. My mother didn't think so either."

"Did she chew you out?"

"No, she took it in stride. Even offered to spring for a trip to the salon to undo it, but of course, that would have meant admitting it was a mistake, so I said no."

"She sounds like a great mom."

"She was. I miss her."

Kris looked down at her teacup. For a second I thought she would say something, then her face hardened.

I wondered why she'd chosen to come to Santa Fe, away from her family. Youthful rebellion? Something a little more permanent than that, I thought. There must have been some deep conflict with her parents, and I wished she would talk about it, but she had never opened up to me about her past. All I knew was that she had moved here, far away from her home, and changed her name.

"Kris, has something else been bothering you? Forgive me, but you seem kind of tense lately."

She pressed her lips together, then sighed. "This isn't the first time kids have shown up at one of our parties."

"Oh."

"And yes, I'm well aware that it's breaking the law. I don't know who's passing the word. I wish they'd stop."

"Sounds like it's time to have a talk with your friends."

"Or find new ones." Her voice was sullen and she frowned as she stuffed the rest of her scone into her mouth and chomped.

"Well, you are having that dinner party here," I said. "There shouldn't be any uninvited guests at that. Maybe it would be an opportunity to discuss the problem."

She nodded, looking thoughtful. "Yeah. You're right, I have to say something."

"Not fun, but easier than finding a whole new set of friends."

"Yeah." She sighed. "Thanks, Ellen."

"Sure. May I ask a favor in return?"

She gave me a wary look. "OK."

"No absinthe at the dinner party. Our beer and wine license won't cover it. Assuming we get the license by then..."

"It's legal if we brown-bag it."

"Please, Kris."

Her shoulders slumped. "OK."

"Thank you."

She picked up her teacup, took a swallow, and cradled the cup in her hands. "They took my fingerprints and everything. I have an arrest record now."

"Well, maybe you won't have a conviction."

"Hope not." She took another sip of tea, then put down the cup and finished her scone. "I'll pay you back the bond money."

"Thank you. Monday morning would be good, if you can manage it."

"I can get it tonight, if you want."

"No need. Monday's soon enough."

"Sorry I had to impose on you."

"It's all right. Of course, I'm legally obligated to nag you to go to your court hearing."

She smiled weakly at the joke, then gazed at the table between us, blinking. "I guess I'm ready to go get my car. I can call a cab—"

"No, don't be silly. I'll drive you."

She collected her purse and the manila envelope from the sideboard. The latter gave a metallic chink as she picked it up. Jewelry, I supposed.

We went back out to the car, and Kris directed me to an older neighborhood on the west side of town. I had pictured the Goth party in one of the Victorians, but those were all downtown and hideously expensive, not the sort of place most Goth kids could afford. I could barely afford it myself, and that was with sinking all my inheritance into it.

The house we stopped at was a cheap cinder-block Pueblo style that was stuccoed, as near as I could tell in the dark, a sickly mint green. I pulled up behind Kris's car—a black Scion —at the curb out in front. There were no lights on in the house, nor any illumination on the porch.

"Did the others all get bailed out?" I asked.

"Yeah. They called their families."

I felt a pang of worry but refrained from telling her to be careful or saying anything else mom-like. Despite the evening's events, Kris wasn't stupid.

"I'll see you on Monday, then," I said.

"Yeah." Kris opened her door and slid out of the car, then bent down to look at me. "Thanks again, Ellen."

"You're welcome. Take care."

She nodded, smiled crookedly, and walked to her own car. I waited just in case she had trouble with it, but it started smoothly and glided away down the street, tires intact and lights all lighting as they should.

I looked at the dashboard clock. Eleven-thirty. Felt more like three a.m.

I drove back to the tearoom, wondering whether to take a hot bath or just collapse. I slowed as I drove up the alley to the back of the house. Something was bothering me, but I didn't figure it out until I turned off the car and the headlights.

Once again, the tearoom was dark. I rolled down my window and listened a little to see if Captain Dusenberry had also turned off the stereo.

No music, but I heard rustling and the sound of smothered laughter.

14

I sat wondering if I should call the police. If, as I suspected, the Goth kids were back under my lilacs, I could legitimately complain about trespass.

I didn't want to be a boring establishment spoilsport—I'd already been that tonight and it wasn't fun—but the thought that they might be imbibing absinthe and who knew what else beneath my lilacs decided me. I took out the flashlight again and quietly got out of my car.

Silence. I stepped up onto the *portal* as if to open the back door, but instead turned to my right and aimed the flash at the bushes.

Three startled faces turned toward me, pale in the harsh light. The next instant they scrambled away, toward the street again. I followed and saw the last one jump the fence and run off uphill. Returning, I shone my light under the bushes and noticed a fleck of white.

I stepped closer and peered at the ground where the kids had been sitting. The white was the tiny stub-end of a roach. A hint of pot smoke lingered in the air.

I looked all around the area but didn't see anything else. Leaving the roach where it was, I called the police department's non-emergency number to report the trespass and request a patrol for the following night.

"Do you want us to send someone now?" asked the dispatcher who answered my call.

"Only if they want to pick up this roach. I doubt the kids will be back tonight."

"We'll assign a patrol for tomorrow. What's the address?"

I gave it, thanked the dispatcher, and hung up. Put away the flashlight and as I set foot on the *portal* again, the dining parlor lights came on.

"You don't seem very friendly to our garden guests," I said as I let myself in.

The lights flickered. I confess it scared me just a little.

"Well, you're right. They weren't invited."

I locked up and went upstairs, leaving Captain Dusenberry to hold the fort. Too tense to sleep right away, I fixed myself a cup of hot milk with cinnamon and drank it at my desk while I surfed up the details of Maria's funeral.

Her obituary was online, and I learned that she was a leading figure in the Hispanic community, so much so that her funeral would be held in St. Francis Basilica, the largest Catholic church in town, and one of Santa Fe's famous landmarks. It spoke to Maria's stature that her funeral was being held there; the cathedral (as I still thought of it) was the center of Santa Fe's Catholic community. I sipped my milk as I read through the details of an amazing life and legacy.

Maria's family had come to New Mexico with the second wave of Spanish settlers in the late seventeenth century. They had been in Santa Fe ever since, and to call them a dynasty would not be exaggerating that much. In addition to the restaurants, which were a fairly new acquisition, having been purchased by Maria's father, she owned quite a lot of real estate and several retail businesses, from a gallery of native art to a haute couture shop on the Plaza. She was the modern equivalent of nobility.

I ordered a large vase of white roses to be sent to the funeral, and wrote a formal note of condolence to Rick and his family. By that time I was yawning, so I shut down my computer and went to bed.

In the morning I slept late, then got up and puttered around the tearoom, laundering linens and aprons and refreshing the vases, pulling out tired flowers and trimming stems. I enjoyed these quiet times when the tearoom was closed and I could walk through the parlors, admiring everything, soaking up the atmosphere of peace and rich beauty. A time to remind myself of what I was trying to create, for myself and for my customers.

I fixed an omelette for brunch and debated what to do with my afternoon. A visit of condolence to Rosa's family? Maybe, but Ricardo might have his hands full with the restaurant at midday on Sunday, unless he could leave it in the hands of a junior manager.

I thought about calling Willow to ask about researching Captain Dusenberry's murder, but the archives and probably the museum offices would be closed. Library, too.

I could follow up with the Rose Guild. An echo of remembered annoyance with Tony spurred me to get out Joan Timothy's card and make a call. She answered on the third ring.

"Hello, Joan, this is Ellen Rosings. I was wondering if this would be a good time to talk a little more about the Rose Guild?"

"Actually I'm on my way to the City Rose Garden. We meet there every weekend to prune and feed. Would you like to join us? We could talk there."

"I'd love to."

"Bring a hat and gloves," she said cheerily. "I'll be over there in about twenty minutes."

"See you there."

I hung up and looked at the shorts and sandals I was wearing. Jeans would be better in a rose garden, as I had no desire to scratch up my thighs. I went upstairs and changed, putting on a light long-sleeved shirt against sunburn and trading the sandals for my garden clogs. Armed with a straw hat, a bottle of ice water, and my gloves and shears in case I was invited to help, I headed out.

The City Rose Garden is actually a park, nicely landscaped with paths, arched bowers over hidden benches, and a central fountain. Lots of people were strolling there on a sunny Sunday afternoon. I saw a cluster of a dozen or more women dressed much as I was at one end of the park, and headed over to join them.

If not for the clothing, I'd have thought they were all likely to be headed for the Wisteria Tearoom. The profile of my average customer is female, over thirty, and Caucasian, and they all fit the bill.

Joining the Rose Guild suddenly seemed an even better idea. I was a little young for the profile, but I'd always hung around with people mostly older than me. I liked roses, and it couldn't hurt to rub elbows with potential customers.

Said potential customers at the moment were busy clipping faded blooms, tying up climbers, doing all the little maintenance chores that kept the roses looking their best. I spotted Joan's tall form and headed toward her.

"Good afternoon!" she said, smiling as she straightened from trimming a burgeoning Mr. Lincoln. She wore a practical hat, a white blouse open over a red t-shirt, and cotton duck trousers of olive green, the knees darkened with dirt.

"Aha, you brought shears—I'm going to put to you work!"

"Please do," I said, smiling.

"There's an Elegant Lady over here that needs some attention."

"That's the Diana, Princess of Wales rose, isn't it?"

"Yes. I don't know why they changed the name. Here it is." She stopped before a tea rose bearing pale white blossoms with just a blush of pink to them.

"Oh, how lovely!" I said, stooping to cup a blossom in my hand and inhale the delicate fragrance. "I thought about planting one but they're hard to find."

"They're temperamental, too, I'm afraid," said Joan. "I'm almost sorry we planted it, except the blooms are so beautiful. Just deadhead and put the trimmings in that milk crate over there."

I started cutting off the faded blooms, clipping each stem back to just above a five-lobed leaf to encourage a new bud to form. Joan watched me for a moment, then went back to her Mr. Lincoln. I smiled to myself, knowing I'd passed initial inspection.

It was soothing, working with the roses, surrounded by their scent and by the gentle, fussy voices of the Rose Guild. I noticed Lucy Kingston a few feet away, pruning a China rose and chattering happily with another woman I didn't recognize. She seemed so cheerful, it was hard to imagine this was the same woman who had exhibited such revulsion at the mention of Maria Garcia's name.

How much money had Mrs. Garcia left the Rose Guild? I couldn't imagine it being worthwhile to kill her for any sum, but the minds of criminals do not see such things normally. I mused about what could inspire a nice old lady to commit murder. By the time I'd finished trimming the Princess Diana, I had reached no conclusion.

It might all be nonsense anyway. It was just as likely— probably more likely—that Mrs. Garcia had picked up the botulism from the soil, perhaps in her own garden.

Except she'd been in the hospital with a broken hip. I remembered the walker she'd used to get into the tearoom, and how weak she had seemed, almost strokey. Had she even gone back to gardening since she'd come home? I'd have been willing to bet she hadn't. Maybe I'd ask Rosa.

I collected my trimmings and carried them to the milk crate Joan had indicated. Lucy Kingston arrived simultaneously with her own double-handful of deadheads. She peered at me from beneath the wide brim of her straw hat, frowning slightly as if trying to remember me. I smiled.

"Hello, Ms. Kingston. Ellen Rosings, from the tearoom?"

"Oh, yes! How nice to see you. Are you joining the Guild?"

"I'm thinking about it. Joan invited me to come and visit."

"Lovely!" She gave me a beaming smile. "We need more younger members. Cora says we should be working to recruit, or we're in danger of dying out, ha ha!"

I didn't answer, a little shocked at such a joke so recently after Maria Garcia's death. Perhaps that hadn't occurred to Ms. Kingston.

"You mean Cora Young, right?" I said after a moment. "Is she a good friend of yours?"

"Oh, yes! We've been friends forever. She's around here somewhere." She craned her head around, scanning the many woman stooping to tend rosebushes, then turned to me with a shrug. "Oh, well. You'll bump into her, probably. I'd better get back to work."

"May I help? I'm done with the bush Joan assigned me."

"Of course! The more the merrier."

I followed her to a bed of mixed tea roses, and began pruning a Gemini while she worked on a Sundance that was covered with mostly-faded blooms. The summer was getting hot, and many of the roses would soon go dormant for a while until the monsoon rains came.

"Have you lived in Santa Fe long, Ms. Kingston?" I asked.

"Oh, call me Lucy. We're not formal in the Guild. Yes, I've lived here forever. We moved here just after getting married. My husband worked for the State, rest his sweet soul."

"Do you have children?"

"Two. They've both flown the coop. One's in Oregon and the other's in Florida, so I have to do things like this to stay busy, ha ha. Cora keeps trying to get me to volunteer with her at the free health clinic, but I don't have any medical background, so I'd get stuck typing or filing."

She seemed so cheery and pleasant it was hard to remember her show of animosity in the tearoom. Being curious, I decided to poke the wasp's nest and see if anything flew out.

"How well did you know Maria Garcia?" I asked.

Her smile immediately closed down, and her lips became set in a grim line. She didn't answer for a moment, being occupied in choosing where to prune a stem. She chopped it with a vicious snap, and threw the spent bloom at her feet.

"Too well," she said in a clipped voice. "I'd rather not have known her at all."

"She couldn't have been that bad," I said.

Lucy turned sharp eyes on me. "Did you know her?"

"Only very slightly."

A wry, mirthless smile turned her lips. "She could appear pleasant. She had lovely manners. Cora says that's how she could work her way into groups like ours."

"What can she have done to upset you?"

Her eyes narrowed. "She had encroaching ways. I don't mean to speak ill of the dead, but she could be very forward, if you know what I mean."

I wasn't sure I did, but I decided not to press the issue. Group dynamics were a reality, unpleasant when they took a sour turn, but inevitable.

I had finished trimming the Gemini, and stooped to pick up my clippings. "Shall I take yours, too?" I offered.

Lucy's smile returned. "Thank you, dear."

I collected the trimmings and carried them to the crate, which was now full to overflowing. Stuffing my contribution on top, I decided to make myself useful by emptying the crate.

Looking around, I saw a dumpster over toward one end of the park, near a small shed whose doors stood open. I carried the milk crate over there and emptied it into the dumpster. Joan came up and joined me, smiling.

"Finished? Shall I give you another assignment?"

"Sure." I saw a familiar face nearby, and waved. "Hello, Ms. Young. Ellen Rosings, from the tearoom," I added as she gave me a startled look.

"Oh, hello!" She smiled, blinking against the bright sunlight from beneath her floppy cloth hat. "How nice of you to join us."

"Beautiful day for gardening."

She nodded and laughed. "Any day's beautiful for gardening, unless it's snowing."

"Or windy," I said, thinking of New Mexico's notorious spring winds.

"Come have a look at these miniatures, Ellen," said Joan.

She led me away toward a raised bed of tiny plants covered with a profusion of equally tiny flowers, little bright balls of red, yellow, pink and white. I reached down to touch a bloom.

"Wow, they look really happy!"

"Have you ever grown them?"

"Not successfully," I admitted. "I've received them as presents a couple of times. I never planted them."

"They do much better in a bed than in a container."

"So I see." I looked up at Joan. "They don't look like they need pruning."

"Oh, no. I just wanted to show them to you. There's a Stainless Steel over here you can help with."

"How do you decide which roses to plant?" I asked as we strolled between beds of riotous rosebushes. I kept sniffing the air, catching tantalizing whiffs of scent.

"Well, it doesn't come up that often. We only have so much room here in the public garden. Unless a plant dies, or the City approves a new bed, we don't usually plant new roses here."

"I see. And you probably don't lose a plant very often. These all look wonderfully healthy."

"Thank you! We do our best, though we do lose one every

now and then. It can get a little contentious, deciding how to replace it. The members nominate varieties they're interested in, then the Board votes on which one to plant. We always consider the variety that was lost, of course. But there are also always wonderful new roses coming out."

"What's the newest rose in the garden?"

"An Our Lady of Guadalupe rose. That was a fight! I almost wanted to resign, it got so bitter!"

"Really? Why?"

"We'd lost a Judy Garland, and Lucy wanted to replace it with another, but Maria nominated the Our Lady of Guadalupe. That's a fairly new variety, named in honor of the Pope recognizing the Virgin of Guadalupe as the patron of the Americas a few years back, you remember?"

I nodded. The Virgin of Guadalupe is a powerful symbol in New Mexico, one I've always been fond of though I'm not a Catholic.

"I didn't know there was a rose named for her."

"Appropriate, don't you think? With the legend and all."

"Yes, indeed." La Guadalupana was famous for a miracle involving roses, and she was often depicted surrounded by them.

"Well, Cora sided with Lucy, and they argued and argued. The other board members were mostly just terrified to even say a thing! The vote came in tied, and I had the tie-breaker. I chose the Our Lady of Guadalupe."

"Why?"

Joan stopped walking and glanced around. A troubled frown had creased her brow.

"Maria had been such a good member for so long," she said quietly. "She was our Vice President, and she made large donations to the Guild every year, over and above her membership. And I felt sorry for her."

Joan started walking again, so briskly I had to hurry to

catch up. I wanted to ask why she felt sorry for Maria Garcia, though I had my suspicions. Maria had been wealthy and powerful and certainly a strong-minded woman, good qualities that might also get one in political trouble.

"May I see the Our Lady of Guadalupe rose?" I asked instead.

"Of course. It's over this way."

She turned down a different path, toward the far corner of the park. I followed her to one of the outer beds, where we found Cora vigorously spraying water onto a large floribunda covered with pink blossoms.

"Easy, Cora!" said Joan. "You're going to blast the petals right off it!"

Cora tuned the hose away and twisted the nozzle to lower the water pressure. "Sorry," she said in a slightly grumpy tone. "It's got aphids."

"Well, it needs feeding anyway. Get some of the systemic. It's in the shed."

Cora nodded and shut off the hose, but stood frowning at the pink rosebush for a moment before dropping the hose on the sidewalk a few feet away. She glanced at me, then shuffled off down another path toward the shed.

"This is it," Joan said, indicating the bush Cora had been hosing down. "Not looking its best at the moment, I'm afraid. I don't know what Cora was thinking."

A number of petals were scattered on the ground beneath the rosebush, and water dripped off of the drooping pink blooms. I didn't bother trying to smell one, as the scent wouldn't be very strong after the hosing.

This was the bush Maria had fought for. Our Lady of Guadalupe. A simple pink rose, nothing extraordinary, but I knew that because of its name it would mean a lot to Maria Garcia.

"Thank you," I said. "I'll come visit it again when it hasn't just had a shower."

Joan smiled. "Come on. I'll help you with the Stainless Steel."

I spent another hour or so pruning roses and chatting with Joan. She introduced me to several of the other ladies, very kindly mentioning my tearoom as she did so, and the ladies made polite interested noises. Very promising.

At mid-afternoon the Rose Guild began winding down its session for the week, for which I was secretly grateful as it was getting rather warm. I helped Joan gather equipment and supplies into a wheelbarrow, which she then rolled to the shed to put away.

"Thanks for visiting us, Ellen."

"Thank you for letting me tag along. I'm very interested in joining the Guild. Do you have a brochure?"

"Oh, I should, shouldn't I? There might be one buried in my the car somewhere—or you can just visit the website."

"That's fine," I said.

"It's santaferoseguild.org," Joan said. "It's on the card I gave you, if you have trouble remembering."

"Great. Thanks again!"

We removed our gardening gloves and shook hands. I rather liked Joan, and I thought my Aunt Nat might like her too. I looked forward to continuing the acquaintance.

"I'll be calling you about the reception," Joan said. "I'm going to want that sample menu, and a quote to put before the board. We meet Thursday."

"All right. We're closed tomorrow, but if you call on Tuesday I should be able to get you a quote by—say, Wednesday morning?"

"Perfect."

Joan pushed the wheelbarrow into the shed, then bid me a cheerful farewell. I strolled off to my car, pleasantly tired and ready for a glass of something cold.

Driving home, I thought about Maria Garcia and her Our Lady of Guadalupe rosebush, and wondered if she had planted one in her own garden. If she even had a garden.

I remembered Tony mentioning she had lived in Casa de Sónset, an upscale assisted living place, a retirement community for people with money. She wouldn't have a garden to play in there. The Rose Guild was probably her only outlet for gardening, then. No wonder she had been willing to fight for the Our Lady of Guadalupe rose.

I parked and went in the tearoom's back door, leaving my gloves and shears on the bench out back with the intention of putting them away later. I wanted a cold drink and a shower before I put things away and figured out what to fix for dinner. Before I even reached the stairs, though, the front doorbell rang.

I considered ignoring it, but couldn't. It might just be someone looking for tea, but it could also be a friend or a neighbor—Katie Hutchins, who ran the B&B across the street, often dropped by to say hello. I left my hat hanging from the bannister post and went to the door, but stopped short as I reached it.

Standing to one side, looking at me through the lights, was Tony Aragón.

15

An echo of the previous night's anger arose, and I almost turned my back, but Tony had seen me and I couldn't be that rude. Instead I opened the door, not caring, for once, how disheveled I might look.

"Hi," he said, holding out a plastic bag containing several pieces of china. "I brought back your things from the lab. The food all tested negative, of course."

I accepted the bag, looking down at the china that had served Maria Garcia's last meal. "Thank you."

"Still mad?"

I glanced up at him. An apprehensive smile hovered on his lips. I took a deep breath.

"Less so."

The smile broadened. "Good."

"I gather she talked back to the officers. She should have known better."

"Yeah."

We stood staring at each other for a long, silent moment. He had on a black t-shirt and jeans, his normal attire. He looked good, and a little anxious as well, which was endearing, much to my annoyance. I didn't want to be attracted to him. I wanted to stay mad, but I just didn't have the energy at the moment.

"Would you like a glass of lemonade?" I said finally.

"That sounds...safe. Good, I mean," he said, laughing at my frown. "It sounds good. Yes, I'd love a glass of lemonade."

I pushed the door open a little wider. "You can come in while I fix it."

He didn't move. "I brought you something else."

"Oh?" I said, trying not to sound too haughty.

He smiled and gestured to his right. "Want to see?"

I stepped out and looked toward the south end of the *portal*. Next to the nearest wicker chair, where he'd apparently been sitting waiting for my return, stood two four-foot columns of wood, carved in the twisted style common to old Spanish furniture and each topped with a white pillar candle.

"Oh! They're beautiful!"

I stepped forward to look more closely at them. They were stained a dark mahogany, and while they looked rough-hewn, I could see that they'd been carefully finished. For an instant I wondered if Tony had made them, but he wouldn't have had time since the night before, and he didn't seem like the type to have a hobby.

He stepped up beside me. "I thought they'd look nice in your—room."

I glanced at him. "Yes, they'd go perfectly with the Renaissance decor. But you shouldn't have."

"I just wanted to say I was sorry. I'm not good at speeches."

He said it lightly, but the look on his face was genuinely anxious. I relented, and smiled.

"Well, thank you. They're lovely."

He smiled back, looking relieved. "Should I bring them in?"

"Yes, please."

He handed me the candles and picked up both pillars. I held open the door, struggling with a moment's reluctance to invite him upstairs. The pillars would have to go up there eventually, though, and the lemonade was in my kitchenette. I locked the front door behind us, dashed to the kitchen to leave the china, then led the way upstairs, grabbing my straw hat along the way.

"Looks like you were out hiking."

"No, I went to visit the Rose Guild. They were working in

the City Rose Garden."

I waited for him to object or criticize, but he was wise enough to keep quiet. I opened the door to my suite and welcomed him in with a gesture.

"Where do you want these?"

"I don't know yet. By the chimney is fine for now."

He set the pillars together beside the chimney that protrudes through the center of my suite and acts as a partial divider. I put the candles on top of them and invited Tony to sit down while I fixed the lemonade.

"Let me guess. You hand-squeeze the lemons."

I hung my hat on the coat rack, then took out a couple of glasses and filled them with ice from my mini-freezer. "That's tearoom thinking. On my own time I'm lazy and use frozen."

"Works for me."

Just to be contrary, I added a slice of fresh lemon to each glass before I carried them to the living room. I sat down in the second chair and handed Tony a glass.

"Thanks. Mmm." He took a long pull. "It's good."

"Glad you like it."

I drank deeply myself, grateful for the cold. We sat in relatively comfortable silence, facing the chimney which I had dressed up with the suggestion of a fireplace. I had found a marble mantelpiece that looked sort of Renaissance at an antique auction, and I'd put it against the chimney with a black backing behind the hearth opening. Above it I'd hung a large painting of a mountain landscape, and in front of the backing I'd put one of those in-the-fireplace candle stands that hold a bunch of tea lights.

Tony gazed at the display for a few minutes, then gave a decisive nod. "Television. Big flatscreen, right where you've got that picture."

"I like that picture, and I don't need a television."

"Oh. Got one in the bedroom?"

"No. I do own a TV, but it's in storage. Don't look at me like I'm from Mars! Not everyone wants to spend her life glued to an idiot box."

"Sorry." He took a swallow of lemonade. "So, what do you do when you want to see the news?"

"That's what the radio's for. And the newspaper."

"Speaking of newspapers—" He dug a folded page of newsprint out of his back pocket. "Still interested in a movie?"

He unfolded the page and offered it to me. I set down my glass and took it.

I'd known I was out of touch, but I hadn't even heard of any of the films listed except for the chick flick Tony had mentioned. I looked at the ad for that one—a long-legged actress who looked vaguely familiar, dressed in a very short skirt and a slightly shorter mink jacket, kicking up one heel and grinning at the viewer. Most of the other movies looked pretty violent, except for one comedy that I suspected would be mostly potty humor.

"Anything look good?" Tony asked.

I shrugged. "What do you think?"

"I'm curious about the mink."

"It looks inoffensive."

"Wow, high praise."

"Sorry."

I kept to myself the suspicion that he was trying to patronize me. What I would really have loved to see was *Les Miserables*, but he'd probably either already seen it or would hate it. And I wasn't sure it was still playing anyway. I looked back at the listings, peering at the small print.

"To be honest, most of what Hollywood does these days doesn't reach me."

"Mm." He drained his glass. "How about a baseball game?"

"Not a sports fan, sorry."

"Except football, right?"

"No, I don't care for football."

He turned in his seat to face me. "I thought you were in marching band!"

"Yes. Liking football isn't a requirement for band."

"So you sat through a bunch of football games even though you don't like football."

I sipped my lemonade. "Right."

"That's crazy. Sorry, but—it's crazy."

"I found ways to amuse myself. Gossiped with my friends. And I stood up and cheered when required."

"You are..." He laughed, shaking his head.

"Yes, you're right. I am from Mars."

"Nah. Venus."

"Oh, quite right. I stand corrected."

He chuckled. "Did you read that book? Or do books bore you too?"

"No, I love to read, but I haven't read that one. Have you?"

"Nah." He shook his glass, spinning the ice in the bottom. "My sister gave it to me. Said it would solve my relationship problems."

"You have relationship problems?"

"No, 'cause I don't have relationships. Not long-term ones, anyway."

He tipped up his glass to get a piece of ice and crunched it. I watched, wondering if he was trying to warn me.

"Would you like some more lemonade?" I said after a moment.

"Sure. Thanks."

Our fingers brushed as he handed me his glass, and he glanced up with a hopeful smile. Disturbed by the way that made my pulse quicken, I hurried over to the kitchenette.

"By the way, I've had some Goth kids hanging around in my garden. They're not Kris's crowd—I think they're younger

—teens maybe. I scared them away last night when I came home, and the night before, too."

"Did you call the police department?"

"I did, and they're going to patrol tonight."

"I'll keep an eye on the place too, if you want."

I handed him his glass. "That's not your job, is it? I didn't mean that you should patrol here, I just thought you'd want to know since you expressed an interest in the nefarious activities of Goths."

My voice developed an edge on the last few words. Tony wisely ignored it.

"Are they acting nefarious?"

"I think so. I found a roach under my lilacs where they'd been sitting."

"Crap. Yeah, better keep an eye out. I'll cruise by when I'm in the neighborhood."

"Well, it's not necessary, but thank you."

He looked as if he was about to say something more, then didn't. I wondered if he was already keeping an eye on my place, and if so whether or not I should be annoyed.

He sipped his lemonade. "You said you visited the Rose Guild. Do they have a headquarters or something?"

"They might, but they were in the City Rose Garden today. I helped them prune roses."

"Oh. Pick up any gossip?"

"As a matter of fact I did." I finished my lemonade and swirled the ice in the glass, considering getting more.

"Gonna make me beg?"

Tony was grinning at me. I put down my glass.

"I thought you might want to conduct your own investigation."

"I will, but it helps to be informed going in."

"All right. Maria Garcia got into a political fight over what kind of rose to plant in a vacant space in the public garden.

Don't laugh, they take these things seriously!"

"I'm sure they do," Tony said, coughing.

"According to Joan Timothy, the Guild's president, it was a nasty fight. She wound up casting a tie-breaking vote in Maria Garcia's favor."

"So they planted the bush Maria wanted?"

"Right. An Our Lady of Guadalupe rose."

Tony's face went serious. "I see. No wonder there was a fight."

"Why do you say that?"

"Our Lady of Guadalupe. Very Spanish."

"Very New Mexican. It's lovely, what's wrong with that?"

Tony drained his glass again and set it next to mine on the table between our chairs. "Nothing. It's just I can see a bunch of old white ladies getting huffy about it."

"You know, that remark borders on the offensive."

He leaned back in the chair and sighed, watching me. "I call them like I see them."

"They're not just a bunch of old white ladies!"

"Yeah? How many Mexicans did you see there today?"

I opened my mouth, then closed it again, thinking back. I was astonished to realize he was right—not one of the Rose Guild members I'd encountered was Hispanic.

16

"There must be Hispanics in the Rose Guild!" I said. "Maria was a member!"

"Bet there aren't any others." Tony shrugged. "It's a white lady club."

"No, I'm sure you're mistaken!"

"They might not say it, but I'd bet money that's how they operate."

I frowned, remembering Lucy Kingston's reaction when I'd mentioned Maria. I didn't want to believe it could carry forward to actual prejudice. "I wish I had a membership list. I think it would prove you wrong."

"Maybe they've got one online. Do you have Internet access, or are you a Luddite about that too?"

"Of course I have Internet access, and I'm not a Luddite! I'm amazed you know the term."

"Now, that is offensive," he said.

"I don't mean because of your race!"

"No, you mean because of my background, which is almost the same thing."

He was glaring at me now. Not the cop glare, though there were echoes of that in it. This was the oversensitive non-college-graduate glare. It worried me.

"I'm surprised you know it because most people don't," I said quietly. "Regardless of race or background."

His face relaxed a little, though there was still a tightness around his jaw. "Fine. Let's fire up your computer and look up the Rose Guild."

"All right."

I led him across the hall to my office, and turned on the computer. He stood next to my chair while I brought up the Rose Guild's website.

"No membership list," I said, looking at the menu.

"Try that link that says 'Thanks to our donors.'"

I clicked it, and the page that came up showed a long list of names. Tony leaned toward the screen to peer at it as I slowly scrolled down the page.

"Hah. Maria's the only Hispanic name on there."

I stared at the screen in disbelief. He was right.

"Well I'm sure there isn't any policy," I said. "I-I'm sure they'd be welcome."

"Yeah. Welcome, but not welcome."

"That's a terrible thing to say!"

He gazed down at me. "You grew up in this town."

"They're nice people. I'm sure Joan Timothy would make a new member welcome, whatever her race."

"Look at it this way. If you wanted to join the Rose Guild, and all the other members were Spanish, would you hesitate?"

"I...well, no. No, I wouldn't!"

"You just did."

"That's not fair—"

"No it isn't fair, but it's a fact of life."

He was right, and I knew it, and it made me feel terrible. It was a fact of life. An ugly one.

He looked at the screen again. "Go back to the top."

I scrolled up, looking through the names again, vainly searching for an Hispanic surname I might have missed. Tony pointed at Maria's name.

"She's up in the top of the list. She must have donated a huge chunk of change."

"Yes, Joan said she made large donations every year."

"Uh-huh. She bought her way in."

I shot him an angry look, not wanting to believe it. "No," I said, but my voice lacked conviction.

"They put up with her because she spread her cash around," Tony said. "That's how you move up in the world if you're a minority."

"Hispanics are not a minority in New Mexico."

"Hispanics with big money are."

I didn't know about that. There were big-name Hispanics around, in politics and in business, but I didn't know what the percentages were. Tony could well be right.

He straightened up. "Well, thanks for the information. I'll look into the Rose Guild. Who'd you say Maria had the fight with?"

"I didn't say."

I was reluctant to tell him, but I felt obligated. Could withholding the name be considered obstruction?

"It was with Lucy Kingston. She's one of the officers of the Guild."

"Uh-huh."

Tony took out his pocket notebook and scribbled in it, glancing at the screen. He'd go through the whole website on his own time, no doubt.

"Thanks. This is helpful."

"I can't believe Lucy Kingston would do anything to harm Maria Garcia."

"Yeah, you're probably right. Gotta look into it, though. Cover all the bases."

He put the notebook back in his pocket. I sat gazing at the screen, feeling depressed.

Tony checked his watch. "Guess I'd better go. Getting on toward dinnertime."

I looked up at him. Part of me wanted to ask him to stay, offer to make dinner for him, but another part couldn't wait for him to leave.

"Sunday dinner at Mama's," he said, taking me off the

hook. "If I miss it I'll catch hell all week."

I smiled, not quite able to laugh. Our conversation still troubled me.

Tony went out into the hall and I followed, going with him downstairs. At the front door he paused.

"Thanks for the lemonade."

"You're welcome. Thank you for the candlesticks."

"They double as a security system. If the Goths come after you, you can wallop them with one of those pillars."

This time I laughed. He smiled back, and brushed my chin with a finger.

"Keep safe," he said, then turned and went down the path to the street.

I watched him put on his helmet, climb onto his bike and leave. Closing the door, I went back up to my suite and cleaned up the lemonade glasses.

I had no appetite and couldn't bear to think about dinner. Suddenly claustrophobic, I grabbed my hat and went back downstairs, fetched my gardening things from the back *portal* along with a bucket and a large vase of water, and went out front to trim my own roses.

Poor Maria. All she had wanted was to garden, to grow her favorite rosebush. The Rose Guild had accepted her, but grudgingly, if Tony was to be believed. Thinking back over my conversation with Joan, I remembered her saying she felt sorry for Maria. That seemed to support Tony's theory.

My feelings about the Rose Guild were now hopelessly jumbled. I liked Joan, but if others in the Guild had subtly opposed Maria, perhaps tried to thwart her deliberately, then I wasn't sure I cared to associate with them.

Perhaps that was the wrong approach to the situation. Perhaps I should join the Rose guild, and work to change things from within. Was that naively optimistic? Maybe, but it was better than giving up.

After an hour I had a bucket full of deadheads and a vase full of fresh roses, and I was hot and tired again. I cleaned up the garden things and carried the vase up to my suite, where I finally took a long shower.

When I emerged, feeling rather better, the sunlight seeping around the edges of the brocade window curtains had a golden hue. I strolled naked into my bedroom and put on a casual, summery dress.

The candlesticks stood huddled together by one end of the chimney where Tony had left them. I moved them to flank the window, stood back to look at them, couldn't decide whether I liked them there or not. I decided to leave them for the time being.

My stomach was no longer in knots and I was able to face the kitchenette, though all I wanted was a salad. I fixed a plate, garnished it with a couple of Greek olives and a dab of cottage cheese, and sat in my living room to eat, as I usually do when alone.

Gazing at my mountain landscape, I was reminded of Tony's desire to replace it with a flatscreen. He'd learned more about me than I about him in that conversation. Cop instinct, maybe, to give away as little as possible about himself.

I realized I was frowning and tried to shake it off. No one wants frown lines permanently etched into one's brow.

Was it a bad idea to pursue a closer acquaintance with Tony? I wondered, not for the first time. On a superficial level it was plainly a bad idea. Cops were notorious for failed relationships. Tony had even said that about himself, or something like it.

Why, then, was he bothering? Was he just after a quick lay? It didn't seem so.

On another level, one we'd danced around that afternoon, was the issue of our different backgrounds. All right, our different racial backgrounds, to be blunt about it.

There were plenty of mixed Anglo-Hispanic couples in Santa Fe. It wasn't at all unusual, but it wasn't something I'd ever considered for myself, so I had never thought about the possible repercussions. They were subtle, but I saw now that they definitely existed.

For one thing, he was Catholic, at least in upbringing. I could respect Catholicism, but I would never embrace it.

I'd hung around with Hispanic kids in high school—the band crowd was egalitarian—but I had never dated an Hispanic. Of course, I could count the guys I had dated on one hand.

In college I had mostly been too busy. A couple of brief flings had been it. Also white guys, but I'd been away from home, in a population more heavily Caucasian.

Was I a bigot?

My instant response was indignant denial, but in light of my recent conversation with Tony I had to reconsider. There is such a thing as habitual bigotry, I decided. A bigotry of avoidance, easy enough to slip into. One tended to run with one's own kind. It was natural. Was it, however, worth making an effort to overcome?

I had a sudden urge to watch *Guess Who's Coming to Dinner*. Annoying, because the best way to do that was call Gina, and we'd just watched a movie at her place the other night. I could imagine Tony laughing at me.

I got up and washed my plate, then poured the last of the lemonade over ice and carried it downstairs. Too sunny on the front *portal*, with the western light slanting in, but the back was cool and shady. I sat on the bench with my feet curled under me, sipping lemonade, thinking about ways to make the back yard look less like the parking lot it was.

I needed the parking for my staff, but maybe I could create a buffer between it and the house. A hedge, perhaps, to shield the *portal* from the sight of the cars. More lilacs?

The lilacs on the north side of the house were coming to the end of their bloom. I glanced at them, thinking absently that I should cut some for my suite. The fragrance bothered some people, so I couldn't put them in the tearoom, but upstairs I could enjoy them.

A lilac hedge along the *portal*? Hedges were heavy, though, even when something as pretty as lilacs. Maybe trellises instead, with climbing roses? But that might block all the morning sunlight from the dining parlor. Captain Dusenberry might be displeased.

"What do you think, Captain? Would you mind roses outside these windows?"

The captain was disinclined to answer, it seemed. I even glanced at the windows behind me, but the lights were off and remained so.

It was a good thing no one was watching me. I was sitting on the *portal* talking to a ghost. Pretty wacko.

What I was really doing was avoiding thinking about Tony or making a decision about him. The subject was uncomfortable, and I am an unabashed hedonist. I like being comfortable. I go out of my way for it.

So. Continue to explore the potential for a relationship? Or play it safe and keep a distance? The former would no doubt involve continued discomfort. The latter...

The latter was boring. And depressing. And chicken-hearted.

I was more than merely interested in Tony, I realized. I truly liked him. I was on my way to liking him very much, despite his annoying habit of rubbing my face in uncomfortable truths.

I only hoped I hadn't disgusted him to the point he was no longer interested in me.

17

I was out of lemonade, and in fact I wanted something stronger to distract me from fretting about Tony. I went upstairs and looked over the selections in my small, climate-controlled wine-cellar, really little more than a specialized mini-refrigerator. The wine industry must be doing well off of such toys, I reflected as I pulled out a bottle of Chardonnay from a New Mexico winery.

I poured myself a glass of wine, then glanced at the book I was currently reading, but I wasn't in the mood. I looked toward the window and decided I didn't like the candlesticks there. If I lit the candles and had the window open, a breeze might blow the curtains against them and start a fire. I moved the candlesticks to stand on either side of my faux fireplace, and stood frowning at them for a while.

They were pretty, but I wasn't sure I wanted to look at them every time I sat down in my living room. And candlesticks—such huge ones, too, seemed to point up the falseness of my little hearth.

I was just debating whether to start a load of laundry—true desperation—when my cell phone played muffled Mozart from the depths of my purse. Mozart meant Gina. I dug the phone out and opened it.

"Gina, my angel of salvation!"

"Hi, girlfriend!" she said cheerily. "Just making sure you're still on the planet."

I carried my wineglass to the living room and curled up in my chair. "Bless you. You've rescued me from the laundry."

Her merry laugh was just the medicine I needed. I smiled

and sipped my wine.

"Turnabout is fair play," Gina said. "You rescued me last time."

"By the way, my chef loved your tiramisu. He wants me to hire you as his assistant."

Gina laughed again. "No, really? But you can't afford me, darling."

"Don't I know it." I took another sip of wine, beginning to feel mellow. "Have a good weekend?"

"Fantastic. Alan took me to a concert at the Lensic last night, and we had dinner after at Santacafé."

"Oh, I like that place."

"We shut them down. Then we went up to Ten Thousand Waves."

"Hot-tubbing in this weather?"

"Oh, it's cooler up in the mountains. It was fabulous."

I listened to Gina rattle on. I was happy for her, and hoped for her sake that Alan would last a while.

When she asked about my weekend, I hesitated. I didn't really want to talk about my abortive date with Tony and bailing Kris out of jail. Instead I told her about my visit to the Rose Guild.

"Sounds like fun," she said. "I don't think I've ever been to the rose garden."

"You should go, it's lovely."

"Maybe I'll take Alan. He actually likes things like flowers and music. It's amazing."

I smiled, though it faded as I made the inevitable comparison to Tony. Not such a perfect fit, for me.

"Gina, do you think I'm a Luddite?"

"What's a Luddite?"

I closed my eyes. "Never mind."

Tony's taste might not match mine, but he was intelligent and well-informed. Could that be more important than liking the same music?

We chatted a while longer and eventually started to say goodbye. Just before hanging up, Gina brought up the Santa Fe Institute lecture.

"Still want to go?"

"Oh, I forgot to check my calendar! Hang on, I'll go look at it now."

I crossed the hall to my office, which was somewhat stuffy so I opened the window a crack to draw the cool air from the swamp cooler into the room. Leaving the chandelier off, I sat in the darkness and brought up my calendar on my computer to check the coming week.

"Wednesday looks clear. Dinner and a lecture it is."

"Remember to ask Tommy."

"Tony. He may not be free."

"Ask him anyway. Life's too short for maybes!"

I smiled. "OK, I will."

"Ciao, darling."

"Ciao."

I closed the phone and entered the lecture into my calendar. Considered calling Tony right then, and chickened out. I felt awkward after our not-entirely-pleasant conversation that afternoon, and wanted a little more time to settle down before I talked to him again.

Since I had the computer fired up I decided to check my email, then surf a little to price out some climbing roses. As I was roaming an online gardening catalog I saw a familiar name go by: Our Lady of Guadalupe. I clicked on the link and was presented with the image of a familiar pink rosebush.

Maria's victory rose. One of her many legacies. I read the description and learned that the Our Lady of Guadalupe rose was blessed by the Diocese of Los Angeles, and that part of the proceeds from every sale went to the Hispanic College Fund. I smiled, thinking it was like Maria, little though I knew her, to support such a cause.

On impulse, and knowing I shouldn't really be spending the money, I ordered an Our Lady of Guadalupe rosebush. The climbers could wait—they'd cost more anyway, and I'd have to do some serious work out back before I'd be ready to plant them. But this small tribute to Maria was important now.

I clicked confirm before I could change my mind, then turned off the browser and mused about where to plant the rose. I should be able to squeeze in one more bush in the front garden. I wanted it in front, where all the tearoom's visitors would see it. Not many would recognize the variety or care what it was, but I would know it was there, which was what counted.

Voices roused me, distant voices, barely audible but out of place. I glanced toward the open window.

"Is this the room?" someone said, followed by a shush and some giggles.

The Goths were back.

18

I turned off my computer screen, then quietly stood up in the darkness and walked over to my office window, which overlooks the lilacs on the north side of the house. I could smell their fragrance rising up into the evening air. Standing to the side of the window, I caught an edge of the lace curtain and moved it just enough so I could see.

Below, on the grassy strip between the lilac bushes and the house, a cluster of dark figures had gathered. Their attention seemed focused on the two easternmost windows on the north side of the house—windows of the dining parlor.

Call Tony? No. Call the cops. Was this an emergency or not? I decided not, and went back to my desk to place the call.

A different dispatcher answered this time. After listening to my complaint, she said, "We'll send someone out when we can."

"When you can? Could you be a little more specific?"

"If they're just talking—"

"They are trespassing, they may be partying, and for all I know they could be planning to break in," I said, controlling my rising annoyance. "This is the third night in a row they've been here. Please, could you send someone soon?"

"We'll send a car as soon as we can."

I thanked her despite not feeling very grateful, and returned to the window to snoop on the Goths. Maybe the patrol I'd requested previously would come by and scare them away.

Peering down at the figures below, I counted six that I could see: two boys and four girls. I paid particular attention to the girls, wanting to be sure none was Kris. One was definitely too plump, I decided after watching for a while. I wasn't sure about the others.

Kris couldn't be there, I told myself. She couldn't be so stupid. If she wanted to bring friends to see the dining parlor, all she need do was ask.

Of course, she had experienced a momentary lapse of wisdom regarding the absinthe party.

There was much whispering below, most of which I couldn't make out. Also much going back and forth between the lilacs and the dining parlor windows. I assumed the attraction was Captain Dusenberry, though it might also be Sylvia Carruthers who had been murdered in the dining parlor on the tearoom's opening day.

I repressed a shudder at the memory. Unlike the captain, poor Sylvia had not stuck around as far as I knew, but no doubt the kids found the murder fascinating.

Part of me wanted to just leave them alone, let them have their fun, but despite empathizing with them I was an official grownup these days, and had certain tedious responsibilities. As property owner I might possibly be held liable for any idiot thing they decided to do to themselves under my lilacs, if I knowingly allowed it to happen.

I pictured myself sallying forth with double-barreled shotgun in hand, the proverbial enraged landowner chasing away the vagrants. Unfortunately I didn't own so much as a BB-gun. I didn't like guns, and was well aware that many people who keep guns at home end up at the wrong end of the barrel.

So, could I intimidate the intruders without a weapon? I had my doubts. Goths liked sharp things, knives in particular, and the kids in the garden might be bristling with them. Kris had shown me one she owned—a wavy-bladed dagger she'd said was her namesake. Sacred blade of the ancient druids, she'd called it. Very romantic, very creepy. Very Goth.

I wondered what her real name had been. Something undramatic and Midwestern? Whatever it was, she had left it behind when she'd left home. Her legal name was now Kris Overland, according to the tax forms on file in her office next door.

A flurry of excitement below drew my attention. The purr of an idling car engine could be heard from the street out front.

The Goths abandoned the windows and dodged between the lilacs, getting under cover an instant before the white beam of a searchlight lanced alongside the house. I held my breath, as no doubt the Goths were doing also.

The light swept back and forth a couple of times, splashing along the grass, up onto the wall of the house, then across the lilac bushes where it broke into a thousand splinters. From the front, the view along the row of lilacs would be foreshortened, and I doubted the police would be able to see the kids through the multiple bushes. Even from my somewhat better perspective I saw no movement, though I knew the kids were there.

A couple more sweeps and the light shut off, followed by the car cruising slowly away. End of patrol. Thank you, Santa Fe Police Department.

Frustrated, I began thinking seriously about calling Tony, but this really wasn't part of his job and I didn't want to impose on him. I should be able to chase the kids off myself. I'd done it the last couple of nights, after all.

Right. Full of conviction, I left the window and went across to my suite to put on some shoes. Miss Manners, I felt sure, would advocate being shod when confronting trespassers.

I marched downstairs and into the dining parlor, turning on the light as I entered. I head a gasp and a "Shh!" from the north windows. I strode over to the right-hand one and pulled back the curtains.

A girl jumped back, her black-glossed lips in a moue of surprise. Her slim figure was sheathed in a black leather corset and a flounced black skirt. Her hair was a dark henna-red, and frizzy. Not Kris, thank goodness.

Behind her I glimpsed a slender black-haired Hispanic boy in a black t-shirt with an elaborate knotwork cross, and another, plumper girl in a loose dark robe like a nun's habit. All these were the impression of an instant, as the kids immediately scattered and ran, giggling as they went.

I turned on the *portal* lights and went outside to investigate the lilacs. No roach this time, but plenty of scuff-marks in the dirt.

As I was peering at them, I heard the sound of a car coming up the alley. Somewhat unusual at this hour, since my neighbors are commercial enterprises and I'm the only resident on my side of the street. I looked up in time to see the car turn into my back yard, headlights off, tires crunching on the gravel of my parking lot.

A sudden glare of white light blinded me, and an amplified male voice said, "Don't move."

19

"Put your hands in the air," commanded the voice.

"I'm the property owner," I called back, then did as I was told.

The light stayed on. Searchlight on a police squad, I was sure. Probably the same car that had cruised the front earlier.

I heard the car door open and footsteps approaching. A second light—a flashlight—came on, weaker but right in my eyes. I moved a hand to shield them.

"I'm Ellen Rosings, I'm the property owner," I said. "Thanks for coming, but you missed the party."

The flashlight beam was lowered and a uniformed cop stepped into the spotlight with me. He was younger than Tony, probably a year or so younger than me. Looked very stern.

"You put in a complaint about trespassers, ma'am?"

Ma'am. How depressing.

"Yes, there were six of them at least. Kids. I just chased them away."

"Kids how old?"

"Late teens. High school age."

I showed him the lilacs and the windows. He searched around the bushes with his flashlight and peered at a couple of dusty footprints, but found nothing more interesting.

"You shouldn't have chased them, ma'am."

"Well, I didn't chase them. I just turned on the light and opened the curtains, and they ran."

"You requested a patrol, right?"

"Yes, and I saw you out front, if that was you. I didn't

realize you'd be coming around back. I thought you'd gone."

Privately, I thought it would have made little difference if I hadn't turned on the light. The kids would have run the second the squad turned into the driveway.

"Well, call if you have any more trouble, ma'am. We'll continue to patrol all week."

"Thank you."

"You should leave your porch lights on."

"All right." If Captain Dusenberry would let me.

I watched him get into his car and back out, then cruise away down the alley. Returning to the house, I noticed soft music playing.

I locked the back door, leaving the *portal* lights on. Stepping into the dining parlor, I closed the curtains again and glanced at the chandelier as I headed back out to the hall.

One crystal swinging back and forth. A thank-you, perhaps?

I turned off the chandelier and gently closed the door, then shut off the stereo and went upstairs to get ready for bed. I remembered I'd left my computer on and stepped into my office to shut it down.

It was too late now to call Tony about the lecture, I concluded with a measure of relief. Manners could be a refuge.

I'd get in touch with him the next day, after I was fortified with a night's sleep. I went back to my suite and the first thing I saw as I stepped in was one of Tony's candlesticks.

They definitely weren't right that close to the hearth. I glanced around, looking for another spot to put them, but I was running out of options. I didn't want them in the bathroom, which left only...

The bedroom. I did not want Tony's giant candlesticks in my bedroom. I didn't want anything of his in there. Not yet.

I moved the candlesticks to flank the outer door of the

suite. They looked all right there, standing guard. Standing watch over my privacy. I frowned, still troubled by their presence, their Tony-ness, in my private rooms.

I shook my head and turned away. It had been a long day and I was flustered by the continuing infestation of Goths. Things might look better in the morning. I went to bed, determined not to think about Tony, and so of course I thought of nothing else until I fell asleep.

Monday morning I rose and donned my navy dress for Maria Garcia's funeral. The mass was to be held at the Basilica at eleven, and I figured why bother changing clothes when the tearoom was closed anyway? I set my hat, gloves, and purse on the credenza in my office, sat at my desk, and started going through phone messages.

Four reservations which I added to Kris's online list, a call from Hooper Dairy, and a message from Willow asking if I wanted to meet her friend at the museum that day. I glanced at the clock, called her back and got voicemail, and left a message that I could probably meet her mid-afternoon.

Kris came in at five minutes to nine, wearing a lavender dress of fairly contemporary style. She paused in the doorway of my office, looking surprised as she took in my sober attire. "You almost look Goth."

"And you almost look normal. What's the occasion?"

"No occasion." She blushed slightly, then reached into her purse and took out a handful of cash, holding it out to me as she stepped up to my desk. "Here's your money."

"Thanks, but it belongs in the cash bag. There's an IOU in there."

"Don't you want to count it?"

I looked up at her. "I trust you."

She went to her office. I heard the creak of the floorboard, then the sound of her opening her desk drawer. A minute later she came back and handed me the IOU, on which she'd written "PAID, Kris."

"Thanks again for helping me out," she said.

I felt badly for twitting her about her dress; she'd probably worn the light color to appease me after Saturday's unfortunate incident. "You're welcome. And I shouldn't have said 'almost normal.' You always look presentable, and I like the unusual, within reason."

She smiled. "Thanks."

"I haven't been downstairs," I said, getting up. "Want some tea?"

"Sure."

I went out to the hallway, glowing with morning light from the windows east and west. Pausing to appreciate the play of rainbow light on the ceiling from the crystals I had hanging in the east window, I wondered what the upper floor had been like when Captain Dusenberry lived there. I would have assumed it was used only for storage, except that the windows were in the original design of the house. Glass being expensive in the day, windows must have been for the benefit of people.

Who had lived up here? Servants? Tenants? Captain Dusenberry was unmarried, so he had no children. Well, I assumed he had none.

I went slowly downstairs, enjoying the silky feel of the old wooden bannister against my palm and the hush of the thick oriental carpet beneath my feet. Sometimes I had to remind myself to enjoy my blessings.

In the butler's pantry, I put the kettle on for a pot of Darjeeling. While it rumbled toward a boil I went across to the dining parlor and listened to the quiet. The gauze curtains were drawn, giving me a ghostly view of the lilacs outside. Captain Dusenberry made no gestures. Perhaps he liked a peaceful morning as much as I.

I set the tea to steeping, then strolled through the front parlors, just assuring myself that all was well and ready for

Tuesday's guests. I stepped into Lily, thinking of Maria and of her grieving family, whom I was soon to meet. Some petals had fallen from a vase of fading roses. I picked them up and carried the vase back to the pantry.

When the timer went off, I removed the infuser from the teapot, covered it with a cozy, then gathered cups and accoutrements onto a tray with the pot. On impulse I went to the kitchen to see if there were any leftover tea goodies in the fridge. All I found was a tub of lemon curd and a half-dozen wisteria-blossom petits fours. The almond icing was only a little dry, and the buttercream wisteria blossoms were plenty moist, so they were passable. I put the cakes on a plate, added it to the tea tray, and carried it all upstairs.

Kris glanced up as I set the tea down on her horizontal file cabinet. I poured for us both, and brought Kris a cup along with the plate of petits fours. I fetched my own cup and settled into her guest chair, watching her choose a cake.

"These things are deadly," she remarked, picking one up. "Mmmm."

"I love them, too. I usually try to resist, but these would have been thrown out..."

She swallowed and picked up her teacup. "Can't have that."

I helped myself to a petit four. Salad for lunch, I thought.

"Is Julio coming in today?" Kris asked.

"I doubt it. The funeral."

"Oh, right. That's why you're looking Goth." She took a sip of tea and eyed the petits fours again. "I wanted to ask him about the menu for our dinner. He said he'd do it."

"He should be in tomorrow," I said, hoping that he would. Otherwise I'd have to come up with a sample menu for Joan myself.

"We've decided on a date, by the way," Kris said. "We want to have it on the summer solstice. You said we could reserve the dining parlor for after hours, right?"

"Yes. No absinthe, or anything else eclectic, please."

Kris's face stiffened slightly. "No, ma'am. Just some wine and mead. And we're all over twenty-one, in case you're wondering."

"Good. You might talk to Julio about the wines, if he's going to cater for you."

She nodded. "He's all gung-ho to do it. Says it'll be a fun change from the sweet and pretty stuff."

I smiled. If Julio enjoyed catering a Gothic dinner, more power to him. Anything that kept him happy here—and was legal—was fine with me. In fact, I'd been toying with the idea of my own dinner party, now that the tearoom was fairly settled into a steady routine.

I refrained from thinking about whether to allow the wine if our license hadn't come through by the time of Kris's dinner party. Private party; technically it was Kris hosting it, not the tearoom. I just tended to be nervous about the letter of the law.

Was that Tony's influence?

I shied away from the question. "How many people will you be having?"

"About a dozen, I think. Maybe less." She pressed her lips together. "There's some friction in the community at the moment."

"Oh?"

She gave her head a little shake. "I shouldn't have mentioned it."

"If there's anything I can do to help—"

"No, it's just...I have to make some choices."

I kept silent, watching. The frown that had haunted her face lately was back.

"Have you ever realized you had to drop a friend, and that doing it would make you enemies?" she asked.

I sipped my tea. "I can't say that I have."

"Well, it sucks. There's no good option. "

"Are there any that outweigh the others?"

"If I stay friends with her, I could get arrested again."

"That seems a distinct disadvantage." I pushed the petit four plate closer to her elbow. "Is this your friend who was hosting the absinthe party?"

"Clarice? No, she's great. This is—the person who's been spreading the word to the younger kids about our parties."

"You found out who it was."

"Yeah. And if I drop her, it'll get all political."

The choice seemed obvious to me, but I wasn't in Kris's shoes. Maybe she loved this friend. Maybe breaking with her would cost Kris her entire community.

"Can you talk to her?"

Kris shook her head. "I tried. She won't listen."

"Will others listen?"

Kris looked up at me in surprise, as if this hadn't occurred to her. "Clarice would. She still might get convicted because of that—" She stopped, scowling, then picked up the last petit four and ate it.

I thought of several things to say, and discarded them all. Kris would have thought of them herself. It really wasn't my place to advise her.

"Well, it sounds like you'd still have at least one friend, then," I said. "Two, if you care to count me."

She looked up with a startled laugh. "Well, thanks." She gazed at the empty plate, thinking.

I got up and refilled our teacups. I'd forgotten to put the cozy over the teapot, and the tea was no longer piping hot. I sipped it anyway.

"Any response to the ad for an assistant for Julio?" I asked, offering distraction.

Kris shook her head. "Not yet. I'd give it a couple of weeks."

"OK."

She stared into the distance briefly, then straightened in her chair and looked at me. "Want me to post it on the Facebook page?"

I carefully refrained from frowning. Where Facebook is concerned, I am indeed a Luddite. The thought of who knew how many people listening in on my random thoughts, and sharing theirs with me, made me cringe. Kris had insisted a Facebook page would be good for the tearoom, so I'd let her set one up, but I refused to do anything with it myself or to create a Facebook account.

"Sure," I said. "Let me know if it gets any nibbles." I checked my watch. "Time for me to go. I'll be back after noon. I can take the bank deposit then."

I stood and carried my teacup and the empty plate to the tray. Ophelia drifted above the file cabinet, looking serene.

"Have a good time," Kris said.

I looked back at her, wondering if she was being ironic, then decided to let it go. I stepped into my office, put on my hat, tucked my gloves and purse under my arm, and went downstairs.

I could have walked, but the day was already warm and I didn't want to arrive overheated, so I drove the short distance to St. Francis Basilica. I arrived at five minutes before eleven and found it fairly packed, despite its size.

Several people were standing outside the front doors, smoking. One, a broad-shouldered Hispanic woman with short, brassy-colored hair, wearing a black dress with shiny gold buttons, watched me with cold eyes. I gave her a polite smile as I passed her and went through the doors, in a hurry to get away from the cigarette smoke.

Inside the thick stone walls it was cooler, and a sense of calm descended on me despite the murmuring of many voices. The stained glass windows glowed with jeweled light, and candles burned on the altar and around the coffin far at the front of the cathedral.

The pews were largely full. I chose to stand at the back of the nave. The vast majority of those in attendance were Hispanic, but I spotted Joan Timothy, also standing, and worked my way over to her. She was one of the few other ladies wearing a hat, which I, being a devoted fan of Miss Manners, counted as a point in her favor.

"Good morning," I said. "Quite a crowd."

"Good morning. Yes, it is. I can't see whether the roses we sent arrived," she said, standing on tiptoe and peering toward the altar.

My own modest floral offering would no doubt be lost in the massive array of memorials I that seemed to be heaped at the front of the church. I could see a large wreath of red roses and several smaller wreaths standing around the coffin, and many floral arrangements on the floor. Roses dominated, which didn't surprise me at all.

"Are any others here from the Rose Guild?" I asked Joan.

She gave me a wry look and shook her head. I was unsurprised, though disappointed, at the answer. I stepped a little closer to Joan and spoke quietly.

"Maria had trouble fitting in with the Guild, didn't she?"

"I'm sorry to say that she did," Joan answered in a low voice. "Most people liked her—don't take me wrong. But there were a few, a small few, who were rather hateful toward her."

"What a shame."

"It was a shame. I felt badly about it, though Maria never seemed to pay attention to it. With support like this, I can see that it wouldn't have mattered to her."

I nodded in agreement, glancing over the crowd. I caught sight of Tony standing in one of the side aisles. He hadn't seen me; he was looking toward the front of the church. Watching the family in the front pew, no doubt. Standard procedure, probably, but it made me the slightest bit uncomfortable. It seemed an intrusion.

I spotted Rosa and her father up in the front, and Julio nearby. Odd to see him in a suit. He sat very stiffly, as if he was uncomfortable. Next to him was a slender woman who I guessed was his mother.

Just before eleven, the brassy-haired woman came in and stood by the holy water font just inside the doors. A late-coming couple paused to talk to her: an Hispanic man in a crisp black suit accompanied by a blonde, also in black, her long, pale hair in a straight ponytail down her back. Both of them took water from the font and crossed themselves.

The brassy-haired woman shook her head at something the man said. He continued talking—arguing, it looked like—until finally the woman stalked down the aisle away from him, shouldering her way through the standing crowd. He followed, returning greetings from people in the crowd, the blonde clinging to his arm.

The cathedral bells rang, putting an end to the murmuring chatter of the attendees. I listened, enjoying the cascading music of the bells, thinking of Maria. The archbishop himself appeared, accompanied by several attendants. Hints of frankincense reached me even in the back of the church.

The mass went on rather a long time, with tributes from many of Maria's family and friends, and guitar music played by a young man who looked familiar in the few glimpses I caught of him. Rick Garcia spoke in a voice charged with grief, and I found myself wishing I could see his face better. Tony was watching intently, I saw, having placed himself near the front pews where he had a good view.

At last the tributes concluded, and the archbishop led the Lord's Prayer. While not deeply religious, I am able to recite this prayer with perfect, and on this occasion rather heartfelt, sincerity. Hearing the united voices of hundreds of people joined in prayer to honor Maria was rather moving.

Next was communion, which took quite a while, considering how many were present. I watched Tony, curious whether he would go forward to take communion. He did not.

Finally the mass was concluded, and the congregation was invited to go to the fellowship hall where a massive potluck was laid out. Many people queued up to inch their way through a long receiving line and express personal condolences to the family. I felt obligated to join them, and Joan came with me.

As we reached the family I noticed Tony leaning against a wall nearby, and noted now that he was dressed in his dark suit out of respect for Maria. This time he saw me, but gave me only a small nod. I nodded back, then stepped up to shake hands with Maria's kin.

I saw Rosa standing with her father at the head of the receiving line. Working my way up to them through the rest of the twenty-odd family members, I found myself confronting the brassy-haired woman.

20

"Hello," I said, offering my hand. "I'm Ellen Rosings, Rosa's employer."

A spark of interest lit her face, making her look slightly less cynical. "You're the one who found Mama."

"Rosa found her, but yes," I said quietly, acknowledging the unspoken point that Maria had died in my establishment. "I'm so sorry."

A wry smile turned her mouth. "Thanks. I'm Rosa's Aunt Estella. She talks about you a lot."

"Oh."

"She loves working in that tea place."

"I'm glad. We enjoy having her there."

It was time to move on, though I wanted to talk more with Estella, who if I recalled correctly was estranged from Maria after going through a divorce. She intrigued me despite her rather tough exterior.

The next people in line were the Hispanic man and the blonde woman I'd seen come into the church together. I introduced myself.

"Matt Garcia," said the man, giving me a firm handshake. "And this is my fiancée, Sherry Anderson," he added with just a hint of defiance in his tone.

"How do you do?" I shook hands with Sherry, whose cheeks had flushed slightly, making her look even prettier. I turned to Matt. "Please accept my condolences."

"Thank you."

"I only recently met Maria. I wish I'd had the chance to know her better."

"Thank you," he repeated with a brief smile, and turned his attention to Joan, who was coming along beside me.

Julio was next in line, more subdued than I'd ever seen him. He just nodded when I expressed my condolences, and turned to the slender the woman I'd seen him with earlier.

"This is my mother, Eva Delgado."

"Ellen Rosings. I'm glad to meet you, though I'm sorry it's on such a sad occasion."

She smiled slightly and murmured her thanks. I stepped forward and found myself facing a woman in her forties, slightly taller than I with the statuesque form of a flamenco dancer and the posture to go with it. Her black hair was pulled into a tight bun, and her gestures and movements were graceful. She gave me an inquiring glance, but before I could speak, Rosa had joined us.

"Mama, this is Ms. Rosings, my boss. Ms. Rosings, this is my mother."

"Lydia Garcia," the woman added, extending a hand. "I'm glad to meet you."

I shook hands, noting the feather-lightness of her grip. "Please accept my condolences. I'm sorry I didn't have the opportunity to know Maria better."

"Thank you," she said, smiling gently. "From all I've heard, she would have enjoyed knowing you."

"That's very kind."

"This is my son, Ramon," she said, putting a hand on the shoulder of the young man who had played the guitar during the mass. He wore a black suit and a discreet silver hoop in one earlobe. He looked a couple of years older than Rosa, and I saw now that they both got a lot of their looks from Lydia, yet I still thought him familiar not just for that reason.

I offered a hand. "Hello, Ramon. Have we met before?"

He blinked and shook hands. "I-I don't think so."

"Well, I enjoyed your music."

"Thanks."

"Do you live in Santa Fe?"

"I'm going to UNM, but I'm home for the summer."

Rick had finished chatting with the people before me in line, and now turned to me. He smiled as we shook hands.

"Ms. Rosings. Thank you for coming."

"Ellen, please. I'm so sorry about your mother."

"Thank you. Thanks for the flowers you sent, too."

"Oh, well. So many people admired Maria," I said, gesturing to the crowded hall. I was surprised and touched that Rick had noticed my offering among all the rest.

"We're having a small gathering at our house after the burial," Rick said. "Just family and a few friends. Will you join us?"

"Thank you, I'd be honored."

"Rosa can give you directions."

I exchanged a smile with Rosa, then stepped a little to the side as Joan joined the group. She shook hands with Lydia and nodded to Rosa and Ramon, then extended a hand to Rick.

"I'm Joan Timothy from the Rose Guild," she said. "I've known your mother for twenty years. She was a wonderful woman and we'll miss her very much."

"Thank you," Rick said, a little stiffly. "And thank you for sending the roses."

"It was the least we could do. We're planning to place a memorial bench in the City Rose Garden as well."

Rick smiled sadly. "She'd like that."

The next people in line were waiting, so Joan and I moved away. The long buffet was now crowded with everyone who'd gone through the receiving line. We headed for the coffee urns on a table off to one side.

"Oh, my," said Joan with a sigh. "Such a sad day."

"Yes." I tasted my coffee and found it rather strong, so I added a dollop of cream. "Although I can only be impressed at how well-loved Maria was."

"Well, it isn't surprising, here."

I looked at Joan, wondering exactly what she meant by that. Here in the basilica? Here among her own kind? I was probably oversensitive after my conversation with Tony the previous day.

I glanced around the hall, noting that Hispanics were in the majority, though there were an ample scattering of Anglos, a few Indians, and a handful of other races mixed through the crowd. Joan and I found seats at the end of one of the long tables set up in the center of the hall.

"You said some members of the Guild were hateful toward Maria," I said quietly. "May I ask who?"

"Oh, dear. I really don't like to say."

"Lucy Kingston?"

"Lucy's a follower. I love her dearly, but she hasn't got an original thought in her head. Sadly, she chose to follow the hatefulness." Joan shook her head. "I'd hoped to stamp it out, though I suppose it doesn't matter now."

"Do you have any other Hispanic members?"

Joan shook her head. "Joining clubs, at least our kind of club, doesn't seem to be popular with Hispanics."

I wondered if Tony would have found that remark offensive, or if he would have considered it vindication of his own opinion. I glanced toward where I'd seen him earlier, watching the family. He was still there.

"What if another Hispanic wanted to join?" I asked. "What would you do?"

Joan looked at me with momentary dismay. "Make her welcome, of course," she said firmly, and raised her cup.

"You'd face the fight all over again."

She fixed me with an appraising look, then gave a small shrug and sipped her coffee. "Some things are worth fighting for."

A rosebush. An equal chance. An ideal.

Maria Garcia had left many legacies, including an unfinished argument. Or so it seemed to me, but perhaps my imagination was overactive.

Joan sighed and stood. "I'd better be going. I'm glad we connected, Ellen. It was nice to see a familiar face."

"So am I." I stood up with her. "I think I will join the Rose Guild."

Joan smiled. "Oh, I hope so."

"So you'll have an ally if the fight comes up again."

"Thanks," she said as we shook hands. "I can use all the help I can get. I'll be calling you tomorrow about that quote."

I said goodbye and watched her go, then glanced at the buffet line. Still long, and I wasn't especially hungry. I went to refresh my coffee instead.

Tony appeared at my elbow, reached for a cup and filled it. "Hi."

"Good morning," I said formally, Miss Manners's mantle descending on my shoulders, preserving me from embarrassment about our last meeting.

He glanced at his wristwatch. "It's afternoon. Got a minute?"

"Very well."

He stepped away from the table and I followed, strolling with him down the length of the hall, sipping coffee. I waited for him to speak since he'd requested my company. This was a chicken-hearted move, particularly since Gina had made me promise to invite him to the lecture, but it was within the bounds of good manners.

"Heard you had a little disturbance last night," he said.

"You police. Always gossiping."

"Why didn't you call me?"

"I didn't want to bother you. It's just kids goofing around. Isn't that a beat cop's job?"

"Yeah...."

He didn't say anything more until we were at the far end of the room, well away from the receiving line and the nearest tables. He stopped and turned to me. I braced myself.

"What's your impression of the family?" he asked.

"Oh." I was slightly disappointed, thinking he might have been about to say something dramatic about race-relations, or us, or both. "Well, I know Rosa, of course, and I'd met Rick before. I like Lydia and Ramon. Estella seems interesting. Matt seems...lawyer-like."

"And the girlfriend?"

"Shy and sweet. Matt introduced her as his fiancée, by the way."

Tony raised an eyebrow. "Gone public. That's new."

"I had that impression."

"Did you meet Eva?"

"Just now. We didn't talk."

He took a swallow of coffee. "You talked a while with the Rose Guild lady. Did she say anything interesting?"

I didn't care to reopen our discussion of racial equity at this moment, so I said, "Not especially. Have you interviewed her?"

"Yeah, her and the other one, you gave me her name. Kingston."

"Lucy Kingston."

"Yeah."

"Did you learn anything interesting from her?"

He took a sip of his coffee. "Yeah. She hated Maria Garcia's guts."

21

My stomach sank. I couldn't believe that Lucy Kingston, who was sweet if a little feather-headed, could have done Maria harm.

"Does she have an alibi?"

Tony laughed. "Alibi? I don't even know if a crime was committed, let alone when. Nah, she doesn't need an alibi. She's too open about hating Maria. If she'd tried to kill her, she'd have been more discreet."

"Oh. You don't think she might be putting on an act?"

"If she's acting, then she deserves an Academy Award. Besides, where would she get hold of botulism, and how would she get close enough to Maria to infect her with it? The wound was a puncture on the wrist, so if someone inflicted it deliberately they'd have to get close. Or be pretty good with a blowgun."

I suddenly remembered seeing a bandage on Maria's wrist at the tearoom. Tony was right, it would have been difficult to stick her there with a hypodermic or some such without coming in close contact. Even on my brief acquaintance with Lucy, I couldn't picture her getting within kissing range of Maria.

Tony finished his coffee and crumpled the paper cup. There was no trash can nearby, so after glancing around he just kept it in his hand.

"I'm pretty close to wrapping this one up," he said. "It'll go on the books as wound botulism, unknown source, unless I uncover something surprising in the next day or so."

"Disappointing."

He shrugged. "All in a day's work. We don't solve every case. Sometimes there isn't a case."

"Have you talked to all the family?"

"Yeah, pretty much. They weren't all chummy with Maria,

but I don't think any of them hated her enough to want her dead."

I mused on that. Estella certainly didn't seem broken up about Maria's death. In fact I suspected she'd been reluctant to take her place with the family on this day of public mourning, though she'd done so in the end. Could she have hated her mother enough to kill her? I didn't see it, but then I had only observed her from a distance, mostly.

Matt and Sherry had reason to celebrate Maria's demise, though they were doing so with quiet decorum. Would they have found it worthwhile to kill for the freedom to marry? I couldn't guess.

Perhaps I was concocting all these suspicions out of thin air. Perhaps Maria had truly died of an unfortunate injury, a sad mischance.

Tony pulled his phone from his pocket and looked at the screen. "Gotta go. Glad I got to see you. Watch out for those Goths, OK?"

I smiled in response, though my heart wasn't in it. Tony strode away, and I realized belatedly that I'd failed to invite him to the lecture. I considered going after him but decided to wait and call him later, when I hoped to be in a brighter mood.

He tossed his coffee cup into a trash can by the back door, then pushed the door open, letting in a blast of sunshine. Hot on his heels, catching the door even before it fell shut, was Estella Garcia. Going out for a smoke, no doubt.

The crowd was diminishing as people began to leave. The receiving line had finally dispersed. Rosa came up to me, looking composed if a little strained, and pressed a slip of paper into my hand.

"That's our address. You know where Escalante Street is?"

"Yes, I can find it. Thank you, Rosa."

She nodded, looking sad. "We're going to the burial now."

"Rosario?"

Another nod. Santa Fe's oldest cemetery was a prestigious resting ground. Maria would have had to pay quite a bit to be buried there, or perhaps her family owned one of the coveted plots.

Rosa glanced toward her parents, who were talking with a handful of well-wishers, edging their way toward the exit. "I'd better go. See you at the house?"

I nodded and gave her a reassuring smile. An answering smile flicked across her face, then she turned and left.

The crowd around the buffet had thinned, but there wasn't much left of the food and I really had no appetite. I decided to stop at home and just have a quick bite of something before joining the Garcia gathering.

I walked out to my car, sighing with relief at having fulfilled my duty and escaped. Funerals reminded one of one's own losses, and mine were still recent enough to ache.

I drove back to the tearoom and went in. Strains of doleful rock music drifted down from upstairs; something from Kris's collection. I went up and looked into her office.

"Have you had lunch?"

Kris nodded.

I was about to leave, then I changed my mind and stepped in. "You know, there's something you might be able to help me with. Those kids I told you about have been in my garden the last three nights, partying and looking in the windows."

Kris's eyes widened. "Every night? Geez! You mentioned they'd been around once."

"Well, more than once now. I don't suppose you've heard anything about it in your community?"

She shook her head. "My friends aren't into partying in other people's gardens." She frowned, and added, "That kind of thing gives us all a bad rep."

"Well, maybe you could put it out on the grapevine that I'd like them to cease and desist."

"Sure. They're looking in the windows?"

"Of the dining parlor. I gather they've heard about Captain Dusenberry."

"Oh. Yeah, that's possible. There's a certain crowd that's into graveyards and that kind of stuff."

"But not your crowd?"

"Just because we're interested in the macabre doesn't mean we're into trespassing," she said with a touch of disdain. "We're classier than that."

I couldn't help smiling. It wouldn't have surprised me to learn that Kris had clandestinely visited a graveyard or two, in her wild and far-distant youth.

I stepped toward the doorway. "I'm going to grab a bite, then I'm going out again. I can take the deposit if it's ready."

She nodded. "It is. Want it now?"

"No, I'll get it on my way out."

I went across the hall to my suite. I didn't feel like making salad, so I grabbed a raspberry yogurt out of my fridge. Sitting in my living room to eat it, I found myself staring at the candlesticks flanking the door. I didn't like them there, either. Someone could catch their clothing on fire, coming through the doorway, if they weren't expecting candles right there.

I frowned. Was it that I didn't like the candlesticks at all? Maybe I should give them to Kris. The Goths would probably flip for them.

No, Tony would be hurt if I gave them away. And really, I did like them. They ought to fit in with my Renaissance decor. I just hadn't found the right place yet.

I finished my yogurt, then moved the candlesticks into the hall, to stand outside my door. An announcement that one was about to enter a different style. A pair of sentinels guarding my gate.

Kris came out into the hall carrying the bank bag. "Oh, those are cool! Where did you get them?"

"They were a gift," I said.

"Can we have them in the dining parlor for our dinner?"

"Sure. Kris, do you think I'm a Luddite?"

She laughed. "Not even close. A Luddite wouldn't be addicted to shopping online."

I reached for the bank bag. "I don't know when I'll be back. I'm going to visit with Julio and Rosa's family for a little while."

Kris nodded and handed me the bag. "Give them my condolences."

"I will. Thanks."

The afternoon was heating up, and I was somewhat regretting my dark clothing by the time I'd sat in line at the bank drive-up and made my way across town to the Garcias' home. The driveway and the curb out front were full of cars. I parked a little way down the street and walked back to the house, which was shaded by grand old cottonwoods in a large front yard. The front door stood open and I stepped in, finding myself in a smaller but still substantial subset of the crowd at the funeral.

The house, an older home that was probably actual adobe, had the look of rambling comfort that marked a modest home improved by repeated additions. The living room was small and crowded with chattering people, who spilled out through the open back door onto a *portal*.

I didn't see any of Rosa's family in the living room, though I recognized several faces from earlier in the day. A lot of the chatter was in Spanish, which made me feel out of place even though I'd taken it in school.

I walked through and out onto the *portal*, admiring the back yard, which was possibly even larger than the front. A glowing lawn was shaded by old cottonwood trees and surrounded with burgeoning rosebushes. I spotted a bush covered in pink blossoms and went over for a closer look. I was pretty sure it was an Our Lady of Guadalupe. I bent down to inhale its fragrance—sweet and old-fashioned.

"Hello again," said a woman's voice beside me.

I turned to face Estella Garcia, cigarette in one hand and a beer bottle in the other. I smiled and took a tiny step away from the smoke.

"Hello." Feeling self-conscious, I added, "Rick invited me."

She nodded and took a drag on her cigarette. "Want a drink?"

"That would be lovely, thank you."

She led me to a folding table at one end of the *portal*, where a crystal punch bowl, open bottles of wine, and a steel washtub filled with ice and beer sat next to a stack of plastic cups. Something for everyone.

"There's sodas in the ice chests," Estella said, indicating two coolers underneath the table.

"This looks good," I said, reaching for a cup and the ladle in the punch bowl.

Estella drained her beer and took a fresh one from the tub. "Man, I'm glad this is almost over."

I couldn't quite conjure a response, so I just smiled and stepped out into the yard again. Estella came with me, and we strolled over to the roses together.

"Such a beautiful garden," I said. "Maria must have planted these."

"Oh, yeah," said Estella. "And guess who got to take care of them when she was too busy with the restaurant?"

"You don't like gardening?"

She shrugged. "When I was a kid I resented it, you know? Didn't like roses because I had to prune the damn things all the time."

"They do need a lot of attention."

"She paid more attention to these bushes than she ever paid to us."

Estella took a long drag of her cigarette, almost down to the filter, then dropped it and ground it into the lawn with her heel. A tiny wisp of smoke rose up from it. I stared at it, wondering how to answer her bitterness.

"You got kids?" she asked.

I shook my head. "I'm not married," I said automatically, though these days it wasn't necessarily a requirement.

"Well, take my advice, and don't ever get married," Estella said.

I met her gaze. "I heard you were divorced."

"Yeah. Dumbest thing I ever did, marrying that asshole." She looked away, gazing distantly in the direction of the roses, and took a long pull at her beer. "Cost me a lot to get rid of him, but I had to. Bastard would have killed me some day."

"He abused you?"

"Oh, yeah. I've still got the scars."

More than one kind, I thought. No wonder Estella seemed angry at the world.

"Were you married young?" I asked.

"Seventeen. Huge mistake. Mama tried to tell me, but you know, when you're seventeen and horny you don't listen."

She took another drink, then rubbed her hand along her hip as if looking for a pocket that wasn't there. "I hated that Mama was right. And then when I finally went to her and told her I knew she was right and I was getting out, she said she'd disown me if I got divorced."

"She couldn't have been serious."

Estella laughed, a bitter laugh that tossed her head back like the recoil from a gun. "Oh, she was serious all right. She was always big on following the rules. Said I'd made my bed and I had to lie in it. Fuck that, I said. If I had to choose between her money and staying the fuck alive, it was a no-brainer. I think that was the first time I ever cussed in front of her."

Estella looked vaguely around the yard, then drank some more beer. She'd almost emptied the bottle. I tried to think of something comforting to say, and failed.

"I didn't care about the money," she said in a softer voice. "It was her acting like I was some irretrievable sinner that pissed me off. Just for getting a fucking divorce. Well, I'm glad I did it. I'm glad I stood up to her, somebody had to. She cared more about fucking church doctrine than she did about her own kids."

"I'm sure that's not true."

"Pardon me, but you don't know shit about this family."

Estella finished her beer in one swig and threw the bottle at a rosebush a few feet away. It knocked a shower of petals loose, then slid to the ground.

I took a careful breath. "You're right, of course. It must be hard for you to go through all this—" I waved my hand toward the house and the other people "—feeling as you do about her."

She laughed again, not quite as harshly this time. "Funny thing is, I still liked the bitch. Didn't see much of her, though. Never got the chance to...."

She took a sharp breath, then coughed. "I need a cigarette. You smoke?"

I shook my head. "Sorry."

"Where the fuck did I leave my purse?" she muttered, looking toward the house. She glanced at me sidelong. "'Scuse me."

I nodded and watched her stalk away. I felt a strange mix of admiration and pity for her. She had shown courage, standing up to Maria. She'd lost her mother's support, which I could only imagine was devastating, and now she'd never have a chance to reconcile.

She was angry, and violent enough to throw a beer bottle at an innocent rosebush. I believed she had the nerve to be a killer, and certainly she had motivation. But I couldn't picture Estella planning a subtle poisoning, and having the patience to wait through its development. She wasn't one to hide her feelings. If she'd wanted to kill Maria I would have expected her to be direct about it, and to crow afterward.

There was also the issue of where the botulism came from. I realized I didn't know where Estella worked. A hospital? Or a research lab? Those were about the only places I could think of where she might possibly have access to a source of botulism.

I finished my punch and stepped over to the rosebush to retrieve Estella's beer bottle, then returned to the *portal*. I threw the bottle away and filled my cup, this time with white wine.

"I saw you talking with Estella," said a man's voice beside me. I looked up into Rick Garcia's concerned eyes. "I hope she didn't offend you."

I smiled slightly. "No, though I think she might have been trying."

He shook his head. "She's having a tough time."

I moved away from the drinks table to make room for a couple of teenage girls who crouched to get at the ice chests. I stepped out onto the lawn with Rick.

"Forgive me for asking," I said, "but was Estella actually disinherited?"

"She told you about that? Yes, Mama cut her out of the will. Matt tried to talk her out of it, but she wouldn't budge. We both kept trying to get her to change it back. Now it's too late."

"It must be awkward for all of you."

"Only because Stella's being as stubborn as Mama ever was." He smiled wryly. "We want to give her a share of our inheritance, to make up for it, you know. We're all agreed, but Stella says she won't take it."

"She won't?"

"No. She's too damn proud and stubborn. Says she doesn't want any of Mama's money."

"Couldn't she use it?"

"She works in a department store, and I guess she makes enough. She'd be more comfortable if she took it, she could buy a house instead of living in an apartment, but...." Rick shrugged. "Just like Mama. Once she takes a stand there's no moving her."

"Well, I think it's fine of you all to offer her a share of your inheritance. She must appreciate the gesture, even if she doesn't say so."

He sighed. "Stella's a little loco, but we love her. Sorry you got treated to one of her tantrums."

I waved a hand in dismissal. "People are emotional when they're grieving, and she's grieving whether she admits it or not."

Rick nodded, and I got the sense he was uncomfortable talking about his family's personal affairs. I clicked into Miss Manners mode and sought an innocuous subject.

"Your home is beautiful, by the way, and so is this garden. I love the roses."

"Thanks. Mama's roses. Rosa and Ramon take care of them now. Well, mostly Rosa, these days."

"Ramon's in college, right?"

"Yeah. Studying computer science. He's going to be another genius, like Matt."

"Your whole family is brilliant, from what I've seen."

He glanced at me. "Thanks, but Matt's really the smart one. He's the one with the sheepskin. Mama loved talking about her son the lawyer."

I looked at his face, wondering if I'd heard a trace of bitterness in his voice. Younger son makes good while the eldest is running the family business. A cause of friction, perhaps.

"I understand Matt's engaged," I said.

"Yeah, finally. Step up from living in sin. I never could

figure out why Mama preferred that to his marrying Sherry."

"Sounds like she was pretty conservative."

"Very conservative, yeah. She always wore a hat to church. Never ate meat on Fridays. She thought Vatican II was a cop-out."

I stifled a laugh. "Oh, dear."

"Sorry. I shouldn't bore you with this stuff."

"No, no, I'm interested. The more I learn about Maria the more I wish I'd had the chance to know her."

He gazed at me, a smile tugging at the corners of his mouth. "She would have liked you, I think."

"Thank you. I know I liked her."

"Thanks." His brow creased in a sudden frown and I thought for a moment he was going to lose his composure, but he coughed and seemed to collect himself. "I don't think I ever thanked you for everything you did, you know, that day. The day Mama died."

"I only did what anyone would do."

"Well, it must have been disruptive for your business."

"Not as much as it might have been."

"This is going to sound weird, but..." He gave an odd, sheepish smile. "I'm glad she died in a beautiful place. She probably died happy, sitting there being waited on like a queen. That was just the kind of thing she loved."

I smiled back. "If we made her last hour a happy one, then I'm glad too."

He nodded, then glanced toward the *portal*. "Well, I'd better circulate. Can I get you anything? Some more wine?"

I looked at my glass, still half full. "No, thank you. I'm fine."

"There's some food in the kitchen. Help yourself."

"Thanks."

"Thank you for coming."

We shook hands and he went away to join a group on the

portal. The offer of food had reminded me that my lunch had been on the light side. Better have something more since I was drinking, I decided. I went into the house and worked my way through the crowded living room toward the kitchen.

A long, narrow room heavily decorated with Mexican tile, the kitchen was equally crowded. I recognized Sherry in one corner, talking with an Hispanic woman about the same age. Working my way to the counter where the food was laid out, I inadvertently bumped into a young man in a dark suit.

He turned even as I excused myself, and the look of surprise on his face rang a memory like a bell in my mind. He was one of the kids who'd been out in my lilacs last night.

He was Ramon.

22

"Now I remember you," I said, smiling cheerfully.

Ramon's eyes went wider and flicked to either side. Checking for his parents, no doubt.

I picked up a paper napkin and took an empanada from a tray on the counter. "Could we talk? Somewhere a little less crowded, perhaps?"

He swallowed, then jerked his head for me to follow him. We left the kitchen and he led me out of the house by the front door. The front yard was almost as pretty as the back, with shady trees and a well-kept lawn. A breeze rustled the leaves of the tall cottonwoods, making a sound like a running stream. I ate the empanada as I strolled toward a cluster of rosebushes at the side of the yard. Ramon followed.

"What do you want?" he said in a surly, defiant voice when we were well away from the front door.

"Funny, I was about to ask you the same thing. You've been in my garden for three nights running, you must be looking for something."

"We're just having fun. We're not hurting anything."

"I beg to differ. I don't like finding roaches under my lilacs."

He frowned. "You going to tell my parents?"

"I suppose I should. You haven't answered my question. What are you looking for on my property?"

He glanced away and gave an impatient sigh. "Rosa said there was a ghost."

"Ah. I thought that might be it. I'm sorry to disappoint you, but he doesn't much care for intruders."

"Who, the ghost?" Ramon laughed. "What's he going to do, run us off?"

"No, but he's not likely to gratify you with any tricks, either."

He stared. "You're serious!"

"Of course." I took a sip of wine. "I gather you were not. Was the ghost just an excuse to party and dabble in trespassing, then? You'd better find another place for that."

"The girls really want to see a ghost. They're into it, you know? So I figured why not."

"Did it occur to you to ask?"

He stared at me, stubborn, defiant. I sighed.

"No, of course it didn't. Where's the fun in actually getting permission to visit a haunted house?"

"Rosa said a lady was killed there a couple of months ago, too."

"Yes. It's an old house. Quite a few people have died in it."

He glanced sharply at me, and I wondered if part of his fascination for the house had to do with Maria. He was plainly a bright kid, too bright to be trespassing just for the hell of it.

"Do you believe in ghosts?" I asked.

He looked away, frowning. "I don't know."

"If you could see your grandmother again, what would you say to her?"

He didn't answer at once, just stared at nothing, looking lost. At last he shrugged.

"That I miss her, I guess. That I'm sorry."

"Sorry?"

"She didn't like the Goth stuff. I knew that, and kind of threw it in her face. She thought it was blasphemous, you know?"

"What do you think?"

"It's just a game." He was frowning.

"Look," I said gently, "I can't have you and your friends

partying in my yard. Bad for me, bad for you. If I let you all come and look at the dining parlor, then will you leave me alone?"

Ramon looked surprised. "You'd do that?"

"Yes, I would."

His face lit with enthusiasm. "Could we have a seance? The girls would get off on that!"

I tried not to make a face. "I'd rather you didn't. I'm sure Captain Dusenberry wouldn't like it. He likes his privacy, I think."

"Oh." He looked crestfallen, and for a moment, much younger.

"I know a woman who does ghost tours," I said. "She might be willing to talk to you and your friends about all the various ghosts in town."

Ramon gave a one-shouldered shrug. "That might be cool."

"Why don't we plan on Sunday evening? I'll talk to Willow and see if she'll come over."

"OK. I'll talk to my friends."

"And in the meantime, no trespassing?"

"Yeah, OK." He nodded, and I thought I detected a hint of relief in his face. "You think he'll show up? The ghost, I mean."

"Well, if you mean will you be able to see him, probably not. The most he does is turn on the lights and the stereo, and sometimes jiggle the crystals on the chandelier."

"That's it? Man, that's a boring ghost."

"I'm afraid so," I said, smothering an inclination to laugh. "Maybe you should look for a more interesting one."

"Yeah. Well, we might as well do this," he said hastily, as if worried that I would renege. "Then the girls will shut up about it."

I nodded. "After dark would be preferable, I assume. Shall we say nine o'clock on Sunday?"

"OK." He gazed at me, and his dark eyes reminded me a little of Tony's. "Thanks. This is nice of you."

"I'm a nice person."

"Rosa said you were." He gave me a rueful grin. "Sorry we've been bothering you. I didn't know you lived in the building."

"Rosa didn't mention it?"

"No. We kind of figured it out after last night."

Took long enough, I thought, though I kept it to myself. I sipped my wine, which was almost gone by now.

"Even if I didn't live there, I wouldn't want you partying on my property after hours."

His face closed down a bit, and I knew any further admonishments would fall on deaf ears. I took a business card out of my purse.

"Call me to confirm Sunday night, in a day or two after I've had a chance to contact Willow."

"OK."

"There you are!" called a voice from the house.

We both turned to see Lydia coming toward us across the grass. I glanced at Ramon, who had gone pale.

"Please don't say anything," he whispered.

I had no time to answer before Lydia joined us. "Your uncle is looking for you," she said, then noticed my card in Ramon's hand. "What's that?"

"We were just chatting," I said, which was absolutely true. "I enjoyed Ramon's music so much, I thought I might ask if he'd come and play at the tearoom some time."

Ramon shot me a grateful look, then nodded as he handed his mother my card. "I think I could do that."

Lydia glanced at the card, then at me. If she was wondering whether I might be interested in her son, she apparently dismissed the idea at once. She gave the card back to Ramon.

"Well, I'm sorry to interrupt, but Uncle Matt needs to leave and he wants to talk to you first."

Ramon nodded and glanced at me as he pocketed my card. "Excuse me," he said, and turned toward the house.

Lydia stayed behind, giving me a long, appraising look. "It's nice of you to ask him to play."

"He's very talented," I said.

"It would be good for him to get into a more adult environment. The kids he runs with...." She shook her head. "I hoped college would take his mind off them, but the minute he came home he was right back with them."

"Have you talked with them? Maybe they're not so bad."

She gave a huff of sarcastic laughter. "They're Goths."

"My office manager's a Goth. She's very—intelligent." I had been about to say responsible, which was true except for the recent lapse regarding the absinthe party.

"Really? You trust one of them to work for you?"

I met her gaze, surprised at the tone of disdain in her voice. One of them. Echoes of prejudice.

"I trust Kris, yes," I said firmly. "She's a good and honest person. Her lifestyle's a bit different than mine, but as long as she does her job well and does credit to the tearoom, I have no complaint."

Lydia looked thoughtful. "I could try and talk to them, I guess, but they're never around. Ramon goes out with them, he never asks them to the house."

"Maybe because he knows you disapprove."

She nodded. "He knows that all right. I'd better talk to him."

I smiled, then finished my wine and checked my watch. It was getting close to five.

"Would you like some more to drink?" Lydia asked.

"No, thank you. I should probably be going soon, but I did want a word with Rosa. Is she in the house?"

Lydia nodded. "She was in the kitchen a minute ago."

We went back into the house and parted in the living room. I returned to the kitchen, but didn't see Rosa. Sherry was still there, though the woman she'd been talking with was gone. She glanced up at me and smiled, the smile of one greeting a comrade. It made me realize that she and I were the only Anglos present.

"Hi," she said. "Ellen, right?"

"Right." I set my empty cup on the counter.

"I didn't get a chance to tell you earlier, I just love your tearoom."

"Oh! Thanks. You've been to tea, then?"

Sherry nodded. "I took my mother on Mother's Day. She adored it."

"You're from Santa Fe?"

"We moved here when I was ten. Mom and Dad bought a little shop over by Sanbusco and sold antique furniture. They did pretty well."

"Is that where your gallery is?"

"No, I'm on Canyon Road."

I raised my brows. "Big time."

She gave a nod of acknowledgment. "I got lucky. Hired on at the White Iris after college, and when Vanessa retired I bought her out."

"Very nice."

We were momentarily alone in the kitchen. I took a step closer to Sherry and lowered my voice.

"Pardon me for asking a nosy question, but I've been wondering—was Maria unkind to you?"

Her cheeks pinked up, but she hastily shook her head. "Not unkind. She was always polite—painfully polite. I know she disapproved of me, and I think she wished I'd just go away, but she never said so to my face."

"It must have been awkward."

"More for Matt than for me. They argued so much over me,

and I know he loved her." She shook her head. "What can you do? We fell in love. There was no question of breaking up."

"Is the rest of the family supportive?"

She nodded. "Mostly. Rick's a bit like his mom, but he's more open-minded. He knows Matt won't change his mind."

"That seems to be a family trait."

"Yes." She laughed softly. "I said no the first couple of times Matt proposed. I knew it would be a problem with Maria, but he wouldn't take no for an answer."

"Do you find the cultural difference a problem? Between you and Matt, I mean."

I was asking more for myself than out of speculation about Maria's death. I waited rather tensely for her answer.

She frowned slightly in thought, then shook her head. "Matt is just Matt. I love him for himself. The rest is small stuff, nothing we can't work out."

My stomach did a slow flip. The implication that the same might apply to me and Tony was frightening, though there was one important difference: Sherry and Matt were both devout Catholics. That had to work in their favor with Matt's family.

I tried to distract myself, get back to my ostensible inquiry. Polite nosiness about the family's loss was far safer than these speculations.

"You must have mixed feelings about Maria's death," I said.

Sherry gave a small sigh. "I'm sad about it. Matt's feelings are more mixed than mine. He loved her very much, but he's also relieved, and feels guilty for that."

I nodded. All very understandable. From Sherry's demeanor I could not imagine that either she or Matt had had anything to do with Maria's death. I would have sworn she hadn't, and she was smart enough to have been suspicious if Matt had acted the least bit oddly. If I was wrong, then she deserved an Academy Award.

A quick footstep drew our attention. Matt came into the kitchen.

"There you are," he said. "It's time to go." He glanced at me and smiled briefly. "Sorry to interrupt, but we're meeting people for dinner."

"Big client," Sherry added. "Shmooze and booze time."

I nodded understanding. "It was nice chatting with you," I said to Sherry. "I'll have to come by and visit your gallery. I haven't been over to Canyon Road in a while."

"Please do."

I turned to Matt, offering a hand. "I'm glad to have met you, though I'm sorry it's under such sad circumstances."

Caught off guard, he showed a flash of dismay. His grip was rather firm, and I saw him swallow. In that moment he reminded me strongly of Rick.

"Thank you," he said in a rough voice, then released my hand and shepherded Sherry out of the kitchen.

I stayed behind, thinking about the last few minutes. If there was anyone I was unsure of, it was Matt. He seemed genuinely distressed, but could that not be caused by guilt?

Unlike Estella, he wasn't estranged from Maria. He'd continued to see her and argue with her. It was conceivable that he could have gotten close enough to inject her with botulism, but where would a lawyer get hold of the stuff? And while he might be able to inject her, I doubted he'd be able to do it without her noticing.

I was beginning to agree with Tony. It looked like this was not a murder. Perhaps I'd been wasting my time, perhaps even annoying the Garcias. Time to throw in the towel, I decided.

Julio came in, took a glass from a cupboard, and filled it with water from the dispenser in the door of the refrigerator. A son comfortable in his own home, though I knew he no longer lived there. I wondered how close he had been to Maria.

"How are you doing?" I asked him.

He hunched a shoulder and chugged the water. Tense, I thought, but I couldn't figure out a way to help.

"You look very elegant," I said.

He exhaled in an ironic huff. "Sacrificial costume for the matriarch."

"Do you not like wearing a suit?"

"It's not who I am."

Who he was: bright, creative, unconventional. The latter would probably have annoyed Maria, from what I had learned. I wanted to encourage him to talk about his grandmother, but I sensed this wasn't the right place.

"Just a heads-up," I said instead. "I'll be asking you to draft a menu tomorrow. Annual dinner for a club. I need to give them a quote."

"OK. Big dinner?"

"Big group, probably a lighter menu. It's mostly women."

"Maybe a buffet."

"Sure. See what you can come up with."

"OK. Is there a theme?"

I bit my lip. "Roses."

Julio grimaced, and turned to refill his glass.

"Kris wants to talk to you about her dinner, too. She asked me to give you her condolences."

He nodded, then stared into the glass.

"You sure you're OK coming in tomorrow? Tuesdays are slow—"

"I'm OK. Thanks."

OK, but angry, I thought. Why?

"All right," I said. "See you later."

I left him in the kitchen and went into the living room, looking for Rosa. She wasn't among those sitting and chatting. I glanced toward the back door and saw her coming in from the *portal*.

"Mama said you were looking for me," she said, coming up

to me.

"Yes. Care to walk me to my car?"

"Sure."

We went out the front and down the sidewalk to the street. The afternoon heat rose up from the pavement, a contrast to the cool comfort of the Garcias' garden.

"I just wanted to let you know you can take tomorrow off if you wish," I said. "Tuesdays are usually slow."

"Thanks. Maybe I will. Okay if I call later and let you know?"

"Absolutely." I passed Kris's good wishes along to her, then glanced at the house and gestured toward the front yard. "Your father told me you take care of the roses."

Rosa nodded. "Nana's flowers. She always checked how they were doing when she came to visit. If they weren't in good shape she'd start working on them, and Papa would worry she was overdoing it."

"You have a lot of rosebushes. It must be time-consuming."

Rosa nodded and smiled sadly. "Papa wants to plant a rosebush at the cemetery, but they won't allow it."

"Well, there are other places he could plant one," I said, thinking of the Our Lady of Guadalupe rose.

"I don't think he should plant a rose for her memorial," Rosa said. "It was a rose that poked Nana, and that's why she died."

23

"What?" I said, staring at Rosa in surprise.

"It was a rose that poked her," she repeated. "It got infected and never healed. She told me about it, and when they said it was the hurt on her wrist that had gotten the botulism, I realized it must have been the poke from the rose."

"Did she tell you which rose caused the wound?"

Rosa shrugged and shook her head. "Could've been here, or it could've been in the city garden. She went to visit there a lot. It doesn't matter, does it? You said the botulism probably came from the soil."

"Yes, I did say that."

I frowned. Maria had recently been released from the hospital, and was in no shape to be down on her knees gardening. I couldn't picture her coming in contact with the soil. Getting poked by a rose I could picture, but how would the wound have been infected?

"Rosa, when did she tell you about being poked? Do you remember?"

Rosa frowned, thinking. "It was the same day she decided to come to the tearoom, and I know I made the reservation a week in advance, so—almost two weeks ago?"

"And when was the last time you saw her near a rosebush?"

"She comes to dinner here every week, but she hasn't been out in the garden since she came home from the hospital."

"You're sure?"

Rosa nodded. "Why?"

"Just trying to narrow things down." I glanced at my watch. "I think I'll stop by the City Rose Garden."

"I wish I could come with you," Rosa said. "Nana had a favorite rosebush there. I'd like to try to figure out which one it was."

"I think I can tell you that."

Rosa's eyes widened. "You can? Oh, please take me with you then! I want to see it."

"Won't your parents mind your leaving?"

"No, it'll be fine. I'll go tell Mama where I'm going."

She ran back to the house as fast as her long dress would let her. Her urgency surprised me a little, but I wasn't about to question it. If seeing her grandmother's rosebush would comfort her, I was all for it. I dug in my purse for my keys, and by the time I had the car unlocked she was back, with her own small purse in her hands.

"Didn't your grandmother ever take you to the city garden?" I asked as I started the car and fired up the air conditioning.

Rosa shook her head. "That was something she did away from the family. She had stuff like that. The Chamber of Commerce, business stuff, you know. She took Papa to the Chamber meetings sometimes, but she never took us to Rose Guild stuff. I'm not sure she really liked it."

"She liked it enough to stay in for twenty years."

"She was always complaining about it, though. The other ladies argued a lot, I guess. It didn't sound like fun."

I turned toward the City Rose Garden, which was only a few blocks away. Glancing at Rosa, I wondered how specific Maria had been about what went on in the Rose Guild.

"I think it was mostly just one or two ladies arguing," I said. "I've met several who were very nice."

Rosa shot me a skeptical glance. "She said they didn't want to plant her rosebush."

"Well, that's true, but it was only a few of them."

"I asked her to show me the rose after they planted it, but

she said no. Said she didn't want to take the chance we might run into one of the nasty ladies. She didn't want me anywhere near the fighting."

"That bad?"

Rosa nodded and looked out the window. The garden was ahead on our left, full of people as before. I parked in the first space I could find, and walked with Rosa toward the corner where Maria's rosebush was planted.

"Why do you want to see this rose if your grandmother wanted you to stay away?"

A determined frown came onto Rosa's face. "She could take care of it when she was alive. Now it's my job."

"The Guild will take care of it, I'm sure."

Rosa shook her head. "Nana didn't trust them to, and neither do I."

We passed an elderly couple sitting on a bench and traded smiles with them. Even on this warm Monday afternoon there were several people in the garden. I found myself tallying up the Anglos and Hispanics. Looking for balance, an even mix? There were a slight majority of whites, though most of the kids were Hispanic.

Stop it, I told myself. No one's keeping score.

We neared the corner of the park, and I started looking for Maria's rosebush. I didn't see the splash of pink where I expected it. For a moment I thought I'd gotten turned around, then I recognized a Brigadoon rose nearby.

I stopped in front of a gap in the cornermost bed. With Rosa beside me, I stared at the shorn-off stumps of canes that were all that was left of the Our Lady of Guadalupe rose.

24

Rosa turned a hurt face toward me. "Was this it?"

I nodded. A terrible sinking feeling gripped me. Why would someone chop down a perfectly healthy rosebush? Aphids aside, the Our Lady rose had been a beautiful plant. Could someone have hated Maria enough to have cut down her rosebush the very day of her funeral?

I knelt to look more closely at the stumps. They were still green, and the sap on the cut ends looked relatively fresh. My guess was that the rose had been cut that morning.

I stood up and looked around, wondering if anyone from the Guild was in the garden. I didn't see anyone I recognized.

"They hated her, didn't they?" Rosa said.

I looked at her and saw tears streaking her face. I gave her my handkerchief and put an arm around her shoulders.

"No, dear. They didn't hate her." Not all of them.

"Then why did they cut down her roses?"

"I don't know, honey. I don't know."

She cried into my shoulder for a couple of minutes. I held her, knowing she probably needed the release.

I suspected Lucy Kingston had cut down the rose, though I had trouble imagining her doing something so vicious. Lucy was a follower, Joan had said. This act of hatred seemed more like the act of an instigator.

As we stood there, I noticed an older Hispanic woman looking at us from a yard across the street. She came out through a gate in the picket fence and crossed the street toward us.

"You looking for Maria's rosebush?" she said in a

challenging voice. "It's in the dumpster." She waved an arm toward a trash dumpster over by the Guild's storage shed, her face in an expression of contempt.

Rosa was pulling herself together, but was in no shape to answer yet. She sniffled into my handkerchief.

"Did you see who cut it?" I asked the woman.

She nodded. She wore a striped top and beige slacks, and a well-worn wedding ring. Her dark hair was piled on her head in an old-lady salon do. She seemed a nice neighborly type, except that at the moment she was scowling.

"One of those Rose Club people," she said. "I don't know her name, but she always wears a floppy hat."

That could describe half the Rose Guild, I thought.

"She was here earrrrly in the morning," said the neighbor lady, relishing her recital. "I saw her through the window when I was making my coffee. She had some of those big clippers—" she gestured as if using long-handled shears "—and she just chopped it, snip, snip! Then she rolled it up in a tarp and threw it in the trash."

I looked at the dumpster, frowning. I was beginning to have a nasty suspicion.

"You friends of Maria's?" the neighbor asked.

"Yes," I answered for both of us. "This is her granddaughter. Did you know Maria?"

"I knew who she was. She didn't know me, but I saw her come to the garden to take care of that rose."

"When was the last time you saw her here?" I asked.

"A week ago Sunday. She came and pruned that rosebush, even though she was in a walker!"

My pulse started to accelerate. The timing was right, if I recalled correctly. Tony had said that botulism could take several days to build up in the system.

"You didn't see her get down on the ground, did you?" I asked.

The neighbor shook her head. "No. She had a little bucket hanging on the walker, and she put the clippings in there, then she threw them away when she was done."

"Was she wearing gloves?"

"No. She didn't used to wear gloves, not that I ever saw."

"Nana never wore gloves," Rosa said in a thick voice.

A choice that might have cost her life, I thought. Keeping that to myself, I turned to the neighbor.

"Thank you. May I ask your name? I'm Ellen Rosings."

"Alma Chacón."

"Thank you, Mrs. Chacón. You've been very helpful."

She smiled then, transforming from angry old lady to sweet old lady in an instant. "Maria was a saint," she declared with a firm nod, then turned to go back to her own garden.

I looked at Rosa. "Do you mind waiting here for a couple of minutes?"

Rosa shook her head, still staring at the severed cane stumps. I squeezed her shoulders and let go.

"I'll be right back."

I hurried to the dumpster and threw the lid open. A ripe smell of rotting junk food and dog poop arose. Frowning, I held my breath and tried to look over the edge, but the dumpster was too tall for me to see inside.

I was not dressed for dumpster diving. Looking around, I spotted an empty milk crate by the Guild's storage shed. I hauled it over to the dumpster and carefully stood on top of it to look in.

There, beneath a day's accumulation of miscellaneous garbage, was a blue tarp. I could see the ends of rose canes sticking out of one end, and a few faded pink petals.

I stepped down from the crate and closed the lid, then put the crate back by the shed and walked away, anxious to escape the smell. Taking out my cell phone, I looked up Tony's number and called it. He answered on the second ring.

"Yeah?"

"Tony, it's Ellen. You're going to think I'm crazy, but I need your help."

"What's the matter?"

I kept my eye on Rosa, who was still standing by the place the Our Lady rose had been. "I think I've found the source of the botulism that caused Maria Garcia's death. Can you bring some of your evidence people to the City Rose Garden?"

"The Rose Garden?"

"Yes. I'm in the northeast corner. Tell them to wear gloves—heavy gloves."

"Ah...okay. It may take a while."

"How long?"

"Half an hour at least, probably."

I wasn't willing to leave, even to run Rosa home. I didn't want to risk the garbage collectors coming by and taking away the rosebush.

"Well, I'll be here waiting," I said. "Please come as quickly as you can."

"You all right?"

"Worried, but yes, I'm all right."

"I'll be there soon."

He disconnected. I put away my phone and rejoined Rosa.

"Let's walk a little," I said, pulling her arm through mine.

I felt protective of her, and didn't want to take the chance, small though I suspected it was, of our being observed by whoever had cut down the rose. I grimaced as I realized I was echoing Maria's behavior. Keeping Rosa away from the danger of the rose garden. The danger of the Rose Guild.

We strolled among the flowering bushes. I stayed fairly close to the dumpster, keeping a jealous eye on it. Rosa meekly came where I led her. I suspected her thoughts were far away.

My phone rang. Worried that it was Tony with some delay, I pulled it out, but the number it showed was Willow's.

"Please excuse me, Rosa. I need to take this." I stepped away from her. "Hello?"

"Ellen. I'm at the museum. Are you coming?"

I hissed and bit back a curse. "Willow, I'm so sorry. I'm afraid I got distracted."

"That's all right. It wasn't a meeting, I just told Bennett we might be dropping by. Should we reschedule?"

"Yes, please. I'll call you this evening, if that's all right."

"Sure."

I said goodbye, then found a bench beneath an arched arbor of climbing roses, shaded from the westering sun by a dense-leaved tree, and urged Rosa to sit down. I sat beside her and kept watch over the dumpster.

"I want to go to a Rose Guild meeting," Rosa announced suddenly.

"Why?"

"I want to ask them why they hated Nana!"

"They didn't, dear. Maybe one or two didn't get along with her—"

"Then those one or two should answer! They must have been the ones who cut down the rose!"

"Why do you think that?"

"Because who else would want to? The ones who didn't want it there in the first place, because Nana wasn't Anglo!"

I closed my eyes briefly. I had thought of another reason for cutting the rose, but I didn't want to discuss it with Rosa at the moment.

The sound of a motorcycle engine made me look up. Tony was circling the garden, looking for a place to park his bike. I stood and watched until he found a space, then turned to Rosa.

"Do you mind waiting here for a few minutes? Then I'll take you home."

Rosa nodded assent, so I left her beneath the arbor and

hurried across the garden to meet Tony. The sun was hot and I was glad I was wearing a hat, even if it was a dark, solar-collecting navy.

Tony had changed out of his suit and was back in his usual t-shirt and jeans. He gave me a quick down-and-up glance as he joined me.

"Still in your funereal splendor?"

"I've been visiting with the Garcias. That's not why I called you."

He nodded. "So where's this source?"

"This way." I led him to the dumpster, briefly explaining how Maria's pet rosebush had been cut as described by the neighbor.

"Little act of hate, eh?" he said. "Well, it's vandalism, maybe, but I'm not even sure that would stick."

"I think it may be more than that. I know Maria was pruning that bush a little over a week ago. Rosa said she'd poked herself on a rose. It was probably this rose. What if the botulism was on the thorns?"

Tony frowned at me. "How could it be on the thorns?"

"I'm not sure. Only if someone put it there, I think."

He stared at me, looking unhappy. Turning to the dumpster, he flipped back the lid and made a face. "Phew."

"The rosebush is wrapped in a blue tarp."

"Yeah, I see it. Think I'll wait for the techs. You couldn't have thought of this before the bush landed in the dumpster, could you?"

I gave a helpless shrug. "I was about to give up on the whole thing, but then Rosa mentioned that the wound that became infected was a rose prick. Maria had complained to her that it wasn't healing."

Tony's face hardened as he gazed at me. He muttered a curse under his breath, then pulled out his phone.

I glanced over toward Rosa. She was still sitting beneath the arbor, looking dejected. I waited while Tony harried his evidence techs along, then when he disconnected and started dialing another number, I interrupted.

"Excuse me, but if you don't mind I think I'll take Rosa home." I gestured toward where she was sitting.

"I'm going to need to talk to her, confirm the thing about the rose prick."

"Does it have to be now? She's a little worn down by the funeral and all, I think."

He followed my gaze, looking at Rosa. "No, it doesn't have to be now."

"Thanks. I'll be back in just a few minutes."

"You don't have to come back. All they're going to do is fish that stuff out of there and take it straight over to the lab."

"Well, all right. Be sure to tell them to be careful not to be scratched by those thorns."

"Yeah, no shit." He glanced at the dumpster. "Or rather, too much shit down in there. Even if there isn't any botulism on those branches, I wouldn't want to pick up a scratch."

I smiled. "Thank you for coming so quickly, and for not dismissing me out of hand."

"I know better than that."

I tilted my head to the side. "Why, Detective Aragón! I believe that was a compliment!"

A smile tugged at the corner of his mouth. "Yeah. Don't let it go to your head."

"No danger of that," I said wryly. I started to turn away, then felt the prick of conscience. I faced him again, my heart beating rather fast.

"Tony—I'm going to a lecture on Wednesday night with some friends. Would you like to join us?"

"A lecture?" he said, looking incredulous.

"Yes. Microbiology."

"That sounds...really boring."

"It's the Santa Fe Institute. Their speakers make even the most boring subjects interesting."

His eyes narrowed. "And if I suffer through this lecture, what do I get?"

"Dinner afterwards. We usually wind up at Pranzo or India Palace."

"Uh-huh. Who're the friends?"

"My best friend Gina—you've met her—and her current boyfriend."

"So you're talking double date."

"Well, yes."

I stood waiting, feeling nervous all out of proportion to the situation. I was an adult, after all, not the anxious teenager I seemed to be channeling.

Tony gazed at me for a long moment. "Yeah, okay. Do I have to dress up?"

"A little nicer than jeans would be good."

"It's a sacrifice, but you're worth it."

I gave a cough of laughter, this time disproportionally pleased. "The lecture's at seven. Come to my house at six-fifteen and we'll all go over in Gina's car."

"Okay."

I stood gazing at him foolishly, reluctant to leave. "Um, you'll call when you hear from the lab?"

"Yeah, but it could be a while. They're probably closed for the day."

"I don't suppose there's any way to expedite things?"

"That's what I was about to do," he said, gesturing with his phone.

I nodded. "I'll leave you to it, then."

He smiled briefly, though his face had gone back to cop mode. I took a couple of steps backward, then tore my gaze away and turned. Heading toward where I'd left Rosa, I saw that she was no longer alone.

A woman was standing by the bench where Rosa sat. She was facing away from me so I couldn't tell who it was, but she was wearing a floppy hat.

25

I quickened my steps, wishing I could run without looking ridiculous. My narrow-skirted dress prevented that, so I settled for a businesslike scurry that quickly brought me to the arbor.

The woman in the hat turned as I came near, and I saw that it was Joan Timothy. She had changed into casual clothes that went along fine with her hat of loose-woven straw. The face she turned to me was aghast.

"Ellen! Is it true that Maria's rosebush has been cut down?"

"Yes, I'm afraid it is."

"I can't believe it! Who would do such a thing?"

"Who indeed?"

A wary look came into her eye. She turned back to Rosa. "I'm so sorry! What a terrible thing to discover, today of all days."

"Yes," I said. "So I think we'd better go."

I gently took Rosa's arm and coaxed her to get up. She clung to me a little, and I could see that she'd been crying again.

"Please excuse us," I said to Joan. "Perhaps I could call you a little later? We need to talk."

The wary look grew into a worried frown. "All right."

"Thanks."

I gave her a polite smile and led Rosa away, back through the garden to my car. Fortunately I had parked far enough from the spot where Maria's rosebush had been planted that we didn't have to pass it again.

I glanced back toward the dumpster before getting into the

car. Tony was pacing beside it, phone to his ear. I saw Joan standing over by the chopped rosebush, gazing down at what was left. For a nervous instant I wondered if Rosa had told her about the neighbor seeing it cut down, and that it was in the dumpster. Joan didn't look that way, though, and as I watched her a police SUV pulled up and double-parked at the curb by the dumpster.

Seeing that Tony had backup, I got in my car and drove Rosa home, restoring her to the tender care of her large family. I was tempted to return to the park, but from what Tony had said it was likely they'd already be gone. Even if they weren't, I'd only be in the way, so I drove home, went upstairs, and kicked off my navy pumps, grateful to get out of the funeral togs at last.

I put my hat in its box and hopped into the shower. Half an hour later I was much more comfortable in a caftan top and shorts. With a glass of ice water in hand, I crossed the hall to my office, dug Joan's card out of my desk, and dialed her number.

"Joan, hi, it's Ellen Rosings. Sorry I couldn't stay to talk in the park."

"Oh, no, I quite understand. Poor child, she'd had a long day."

"Yes." I paused to choose my next words with care. "Joan, you told me that Lucy Kingston is a follower. Who did she follow the most?"

A long silence followed. I turned on my computer while I waited.

At last Joan gave a sigh. "Cora."

"Cora Young?"

"Yes. I suppose you think it was she who cut down the rosebush."

"I do."

I had only wanted Joan to confirm what I already

suspected. I brought up the Rose Guild's website on my computer. Clicking on the "Board of Directors" link, I saw photos of Joan, Cora, and Lucy, along with a number of others, but no picture of Maria.

"Joan, who does your website?"

"Cora's daughter, Lisa."

"So that's why Cora's already listed as Vice President."

"It says that? She won't be confirmed until Thursday. Of course, there's no question about it, but still...."

"Cora hated Maria, didn't she?"

"Oh, dear. I don't like talking about this."

"Sorry, but I need to know."

She sighed. "Cora felt threatened by Maria. They never got along well, but at first Maria was philosophical about it. I think she knew, coming into the Guild as she did—well, I think she felt a little out of place."

"No thanks to Cora and Lucy."

"Yes. Though in recent years Maria took a more active role in the Guild. I think she just needed an outlet after she retired —you know, running a restaurant, one must be used to telling others what to do."

"Yes, I know."

"Oh, of course you do. Well, anyway, Maria started to putting her name in for the Board. She was elected, and promptly ran for office. She became Vice President for the first time...I think it was six years ago."

"And Cora was bent out of shape?"

"She was furious, that first year! I spent a lot of time talking her down. She convinced herself that Maria was out to get her personally."

I thought that was possible, though from what I'd learned of Maria she'd probably go about it indirectly. She was the sort who let her actions speak for themselves.

"Then when Maria had that fall, poor dear, and was in the

hospital for months, Cora stepped in as Vice President pro tem. She seemed eager to make up for the past—she worked very hard. She took on all publicity matters. That's why we have such a good website."

A good website with no mention of Maria, except as a donor. I wondered if she'd ever been listed on it as an officer at all.

"What happened when Maria came back?"

"Well, there was a little unpleasantness. Cora didn't say anything to Maria directly, but there were little things. Comments about Maria's being too frail to handle the office. I think Cora must have complained privately to Lucy, and Lucy had no compunction about being offensive to Maria's face."

"Do you think Lucy could have cut down the rosebush?"

"I really don't think so. She's mostly all talk."

I nodded. I was fairly certain now that Cora had cut down the bush. Less certain why. Had she merely killed a rose, or had she also killed Maria?

"Thank you, Joan. This helps me understand a lot."

"I suppose you won't be joining the Guild now, after all this."

"I don't know." I gazed at the pictures of Cora and Lucy on my screen. "I think maybe someone needs to keep working against this kind of hatefulness. To walk away is to let it win."

"Yes, but it's hard, when you see a friend behaving badly, to step in and say something."

"Did you consider Maria a friend?"

"Well...yes, but not a close friend."

"Not close enough to stand up for."

After a moment, Joan said, "Perhaps I've turned too much a blind eye."

"Perhaps so. Thank you, Joan. I'll talk to you again soon."

I hung up the phone and gazed at the screen, trying to picture Cora and Lucy as I had seen them in the city garden.

Lucy had worn a flat-brimmed straw hat, as I recalled. Cora's hat had been cloth—and floppy.

As I visualized her I had a flash of memory. Cora looking up at me and Joan as we came to look at the Our Lady of Guadalupe rose. She'd been hosing down the rose, rather too enthusiastically, I'd thought at the time. Aphids, she had said, but what if it had been something else she was trying to wash away?

I picked up the phone again and called Tony. Drummed the desktop impatiently with my fingers while it rang.

"Hi, Ellen."

"Hi. Any news?"

"Nothing conclusive yet, but Kyle found something on some of the thorns. It was sticky and kind of dry."

My heart jumped. "Could be dry from a week in the sun."

"Yeah. Anyway, he's looking at it under a microscope now."

"You got him to work late!"

"Yeah, now I owe him a six pack."

I chuckled. "Thanks. Maybe I should spot you the beer."

"Nah. I'd rather have an evening of your company, if we're going to discuss debts of favor."

"Well, you're getting that on Wednesday."

"Chaperoned. In a lecture hall."

"It's a start."

"Hm. What are you going to wear?"

His voice had dropped and gone sexy. I felt a small shiver of response.

"I haven't thought about it yet."

"I liked that dress you wore Saturday."

"Did you?"

"Mm-hm. Like the way it rides on you."

I bit my lip. "Maybe I'll wear that, then," I managed to say in a fairly steady voice.

"Hang on a sec."

I heard the sound of him putting a hand over the phone, and muffled voices. I sat with the phone pressed to my ear, thinking about dancing with Tony, wearing my violet dress.

A scraping sound over the phone was followed by Tony's voice. "Ellen, you were right. It's botulism."

26

My stomach sank. "Botulism."

"Yeah, suspended in honey, he thinks."

"Honey?"

"Probably to keep it alive a little while. It's all dead now, but Kyle says honey's friendly with botulism."

I nodded. "Yes. Babies can get it from honey."

"The honey could have kept the stuff alive for a short time. If the killer painted it on the thorns right before Maria came along—"

"Dear God!"

The killer. It was murder. I closed my eyes, fighting sudden tears. Poor Maria. Killed out of hatred, because of a silly, petty fight blown all out of proportion.

Tony was still talking. I pulled myself together.

"I'm sorry, could you repeat that?"

"I said I need to find out more about this Rose Guild. Someone in that club might know who could have been messing with the rose."

"There's the neighbor who saw it cut down," I said. "Alma Chacón."

"Right. I'll go talk to her."

I looked at my computer screen. "The Rose Guild's website has photos of some of the members. Maybe she could identify the—the person who cut down the rose—by looking at them. If it's someone in the Guild."

"Worth a try, though it wouldn't make sense for the Guild to kill Maria for the bequest. She was making big yearly donations. She was worth more to them alive."

"There might have been another reason," I said.

A pause. "Such as?"

"Well, you know not everyone in the Guild got along with Maria."

"To the tune of trying to kill her?"

"Maybe," I said, not wanting to acknowledge it.

"Do you have someone in particular in mind?" Tony said slowly.

"I'm not positive. You should show the photos to Mrs. Chacón."

Another pause. "Okay. What's the site's address again?"

I gave it to him, feeling a tiny pang of guilt. I was letting him take a less-than-direct route to finding the killer, but I wanted just a little bit of time before he got to Cora. I didn't think a slight delay would imperil his investigation. It seemed pretty clear who had cut down the rose, and now, why.

"Any other suggestions?" Tony asked.

"Not now. Let me know what you learn from Mrs. Chacón."

"Why do I get the feeling you know what she's going to say?"

"It's just a hunch."

"Hm. Don't do anything stupid, okay?"

"Okay. Bye."

He hung up, as usual without saying goodbye. It didn't offend me any more. It was just Tony.

I closed my eyes briefly. I hoped he wouldn't be angry with me. Maybe he would, but I had to take that chance. I had chided Joan for passively standing by while the fighting went on under her nose. I felt obliged to at least speak my mind.

I took out the phone book from my desk drawer and turned to the residential listings. Luck was with me; Cora Young was listed. I copied down her address, then changed my shorts for a skirt and brushed my hair. Grabbing my purse, I headed out once more.

It was now early evening, still warm but beginning to show signs of cooling down. The sun was just about to set, but I didn't pause to admire it. I drove straight to Cora's house on the south side of town, not very far from the Garcias', ironically, and close to the City Rose Garden.

The house was a comfortable old frame-stucco place, not as large as the Garcias' and probably a decade or so newer. The trees in the front yard were neat and prim, well-trimmed shade trees, not as grand and sprawling as the Garcias' cottonwoods.

The front porch light was on, reminding me that the patrol cop had suggested I leave my own light on. Naturally, I had neglected to do so, but I hoped Ramon would stick to his word and find some other way to entertain his pals tonight.

I parked and walked up to the door. A moment after I rang the bell I heard footsteps, then Cora opened the door and looked out.

"Hello, Ms. Young. I'm Ellen Rosings, remember?"

"Yes," she said slowly, looking wary.

"I'm sorry to drop by without warning, but I just wanted to ask you a couple of questions about the Rose Guild. It'll only take a minute or two. May I come in?"

She gazed at me, frowning slightly, then opened the door. I followed her into her living room, noting the furnishings that had been fashionable thirty years before—a little tired-looking now—as well as a few pieces of equally outdated artwork, some pottery, a Navajo rug hanging on one wall.

Cora invited me to sit down and I perched on the sofa. She didn't offer any refreshment, but then I'd come without invitation. Square, in terms of civility or lack thereof.

"What did you want to know?" Cora asked.

"I'm curious why Maria Garcia was the only Hispanic in the Rose Guild. Do you have any idea?"

Cora blinked a couple of times. "I really couldn't say."

"Joan assured me that Hispanics were welcome, but she seemed to think not everyone in the Guild felt that way."

Cora said nothing. A mulish look settled on her face, and her eyes hardened.

"How do you feel about it?" I pressed. "Would you mind if there were more Hispanic members in the Guild?"

"I hadn't thought about it. Why do you ask?"

"I have a young friend who is interested in the Guild, but she isn't sure she'd be welcome, and neither am I. I certainly wouldn't want her to come into an unfriendly situation."

"I take it she's a Mexican?"

I paused at the somewhat less-than-polite term, and the similar edge in her voice. We were getting to the heart of the matter.

"She's Hispanic, yes."

"Then she might not be comfortable, being the only one."

"Now that Maria's gone."

Cora was silent. I pressed on.

"It's a pity Maria died so suddenly. I understand she did a lot for the Guild."

"Made a lot of trouble, is what she did," Cora said gruffly.

"Trouble?" I held my face in an expression of innocent inquiry.

"Her and her pushing ways. She'd have been fine if she hadn't insisted on meddling."

"How did she meddle?"

"How didn't she?" Cora sounded exasperated. "Understand me, I don't mind Mexicans as long as they keep to their place."

I was astonished. "Their *place*?"

"Like that little girl you have working for you. She was sweet, and polite."

"She's Maria Garcia's granddaughter."

Now Cora looked surprised. I hadn't meant to blurt that out, but I was getting angry.

"Well, that's what I mean," Cora said, looking flustered. "She comes from a restaurant family, and she's working in a restaurant."

"And I suppose you'd object to her seeking some more challenging form of employment."

"Of course not. She should try to better herself. Maria Garcia did very well."

"Except she didn't keep to her place."

Cora looked at me like a parent patiently explaining things to an ignorant child. "You have to understand, most of these people have very little potential. I see them all the time at the health clinic—derelicts, drug addicts, teenage mothers ..."

Something clicked in my mind. Cora volunteered at a free health clinic, a place where sickness and infection were commonplace. Could she have had access to botulism there? Something Tony had said about drug addicts niggled in my brain. I tried to pin it down, but Cora was still talking.

"...most of them will never amount to anything."

"I think it's unfair to judge an entire race by its worst examples," I said. "Don't you see Anglo addicts and homeless at the clinic?"

She gave me a tolerant smile. "When you've seen more of the world, you'll understand."

I'd had enough of her patronizing tone. I was about to take my leave when the doorbell rang. Cora gave me an odd look, then got up and went to answer it. A moment later I heard Tony's voice.

I stood and slung my purse over my shoulder, then followed Cora to the front door, where she was looking at Tony's badge. Beyond them, I saw a squad car parked at the curb behind my car.

Tony gave me a sharp glance. "I see you have company," he

said dryly.

"I was just leaving," I replied. "Ms. Young has been telling me about her volunteer work at a free health clinic."

Tony's brows shot up and he looked back at Cora. "Treat any heroin addicts there?"

"Constantly," Cora said with a glance at me, "as I was just explaining."

Tony's eyes sharpened. "When's the last time you saw a case of botulism?"

27

Cora looked stunned, then her face closed down. "I don't know what you're talking about."

"Black tar heroin," Tony said. "Comes up from Mexico. It's sometimes contaminated with botulism. The addicts shoot themselves up with it, next thing you know they've got a toxic wound. You must see a case once in a while."

"I don't recall."

"Maybe the clinic's records will say."

She looked sharply up at him. If I hadn't already been convinced of her guilt, the anger in her glance at that moment would have sold me.

"But that's not why I'm here," Tony said to Cora. "I came to ask why you cut down a rosebush in the City Rose Garden this morning."

Cora looked startled again, caught off guard by the change of tactics. Tony's expression was completely professional, but I caught the slight twitch at one corner of his mouth. He was enjoying this.

Cora opened her mouth, but before she could speak Tony added, "You were seen by the woman who lives across the street. She identified your photograph."

Cora's mouth snapped shut and a frown settled on her brow. "Excuse me," she said tightly. "I need to make a phone call."

"You can make it from the station," Tony said. "We've got more to talk about."

"Are you arresting me?" she demanded.

"If you insist."

She stared coldly at him for a long moment. Her face, set with anger and, I thought, a hint of contempt, was as unattractive as a woman's could be.

"I'll get my purse," she said at last. "You'll have to excuse me, Miss Rosings."

"Not at all," I said. "I see that I've come at a bad time."

I glanced at Tony, hoping he picked up on my implicit apology. He gave no sign, but he didn't look angry, either.

Cora went to a low bookcase and slowly picked up a purse from it. Something about the motion bothered me. As she was turning back, I saw that she had also picked up something else.

"Cora, no!"

"Don't move!" Tony's voice was sharp enough that I, too, froze.

Cora held a large pair of gardening shears. She stared at Tony with pure hatred in her pale eyes, then her gaze flicked down to the gun in his hands.

My heart pounded so hard it hurt. I held my breath.

"Don't," Tony said in a quieter tone. "You don't want a resisting arrest charge."

Cora blinked once, then swallowed. "I was just going to put these away. Don't want anyone getting hurt by mistake."

She pointed the blades at the floor and moved slowly past me toward the front door. Tony stepped back out of her reach, keeping the gun trained on her. She opened a closet, put the shears inside, and closed the door.

"All right," Tony said. "Come on out."

Cora shot a glare at me, then obeyed. I followed her out and pulled the front door closed behind me.

Tony and Cora walked down the driveway to the squad car. Tony still held his gun, though he no longer had it aimed at her.

A uniformed officer was waiting in the driver's seat of the

squad. Tony helped Cora into the back seat of the car, looked toward me as he straightened, then climbed into the shotgun seat. The squad pulled away.

I went to my car, got in and turned on the engine, then sat with my hands on the steering wheel and the air conditioner blowing cool on my face as I sorted through mixed emotions. Adrenaline still sang through me. Cora's rage had frightened me, but so had the sight of Tony aiming his gun at her heart.

It seemed that Tony had ample evidence to associate Cora with Maria's death. Whether she'd be convicted was a matter for the courts. I told myself I was glad, but mostly I felt an overwhelming sense of sorrow. Sorrow for Maria, for her family, and for a society that could still harbor such hatred, even among its supposedly enlightened and privileged members.

On impulse I decided to drive past the rose garden again. It was getting late and there were fewer people in the park, now that the sun had set. I found a parking place near where Maria's Our Lady of Guadalupe rose had been, and got out to look at the stumps once more.

Someone had placed a vase of cut roses there in front of the cut cane stumps—garden roses, not florist roses. A tall glass votive candle stood beside them, its young flame flickering slightly in the breeze, a small, promising glow against the falling dusk. On the glass was a decal of the Virgin of Guadalupe, surrounded by roses. The wax was pink, and the fragrance of roses hung in the air.

A memorial to a fallen rosebush, or perhaps more to the rose's champion. I glanced toward Alma Chacón's house. She wasn't in the garden at this hour, but I could see her rosebushes blooming behind the picket fence.

Maybe Alma would like to join the Rose Guild, I thought. Smiling softly, I drove home to cut a few roses of my own.

I slowed as I pulled into the driveway. An unfamiliar car

was parked behind the kitchen. I coasted into my parking space, staring at the back of the house. The kitchen windows blazed with light.

Captain Dusenberry hadn't shown any interest in the kitchen so far. I got out of the car and walked to the back door, keeping my eye on the kitchen windows.

Movement made me stop short, suddenly breathless, then I recognized Julio's mop of curly dark hair. He had changed out of the suit into a black muscle shirt and cargo pants. He stood by the prep table, talking to another young man who looked vaguely familiar: blond hair, slender, a little taller than Julio. I could just hear their voices, but couldn't tell what they were saying. From the intensity on Julio's face, it was a deep conversation.

I went to the back door and let myself in, careful to make some noise. I closed the door and heard no voices; the place was silent. Having come into the hallway, I had to walk down it a bit and turn into the smaller hall that passed the butler's pantry in order to get to the kitchen. The smell of baking chocolate reached me.

I paused in the pantry to take out an empty vase and half fill it with water. Leaving it on the counter, I continued to the kitchen.

Julio was leaning back against the prep table, arms crossed, waiting for me. His guest stood behind the table and gave me an apprehensive look as I came in. The table was covered with bowls, measuring cups and spoons, and so on.

"I saw the lights on," I said.

"Sorry," Julio said, sounding almost surly. "Didn't mean to bother you."

"No bother. I just came to fetch some … flowers." I looked at his friend. "Have we met? You look familiar."

He swallowed.

"This is Adam. He was at the grand opening."

"Oh—your roommate? Yes, I remember now—you're a chef too, right?"

Adam looked uncomfortable. Julio stood.

"He might apply for the assistant position here. That OK with you?"

Again, a hint of anger or perhaps just defiance in his voice. I looked from Julio to Adam.

"I'm afraid it's just part time for now. The budget won't handle more."

A shrug. "I don't mind." He glanced at Julio. "I should go."

Julio's chin rose. "No—"

"Please don't let me disturb you," I said, clicking into Miss Manners mode. "I'm about to go out again."

I met Julio's gaze, saw his slight nod and a look of relief in his eyes, and turned back to the pantry. I grabbed the vase and a small pair of garden snips I kept there for flower arranging, and went back outside.

Dusk was gathering in the garden, but I could see well enough to gather some roses. The white and yellow blooms glowed in the evening light. I filled the vase with a mix of colors, then headed back to my car. I decided to cut a few lilacs to go with the roses. I could hear voices again—too muffled for me to make out what they were saying. I got in the car, bringing the garden snips with me and carefully buckling the passenger seat belt around the vase.

It was nearly dark by the time I returned to the park. Street lights were on now, their limited spectrum of light washing out the colors of the roses. I parked and got out, carrying my offering toward the slain rosebush, but slowed as I saw someone else already standing there.

The woman turned her head toward me and the streetlight glinted on brassy hair. I walked up to join Estella Garcia by the dead rosebush. A second vase of roses now stood beside the first—a huge vase, filled to overflowing with roses, no doubt cut from the Garcia family's garden. I placed my own smaller offering beside it.

"Rosa told us about this," Estella said in a harsh voice. "Some asshole cut down Mama's rosebush. Poor little Rosa can't stop crying."

"If it's any comfort, the hateful person who did this has been caught."

"Yeah?" She glanced at me, a hunter's sharpness in her eyes. "Who is it? I'd like to give them a piece of my mind."

"I expect you'll find out soon."

I didn't want to be the one to inform the Garcias that Maria had been murdered. Fresh grief all over again for them, and it would come soon enough. A visit from a police chaplain, who would no doubt be able to comfort them better than I.

"Those are lovely," I said, leaning down to brush my hand along the large vase of roses.

"Some from every one of Mama's bushes," Estella said, her voice now surprisingly soft. "We all went out and cut them."

I straightened up. "Do you still like roses, in spite of everything?"

She looked at me, her face dour at first, then she shrugged and gave a twisted smile. "How can you not like roses?"

I smiled back. A plan was forming in my mind. I would join the Rose Guild, and encourage some others to join as well: Estella, Rosa, and Alma Chacón. They'd represent three generations, for Alma was about Maria's age. It would be a start.

"Estella, I would be honored if you would join me for tea some time. May I give you my card? You can let me know when would be a good time for you, if you decide you'd like to come."

She looked surprised as she accepted my card. "That's really nice of you."

"I'd like to get better acquainted with you, if that's all right with you. When you feel up to it—there's no hurry."

"Thanks." Estella coughed and sniffed, then said, "I gotta go." She started to leave, then turned back and gestured awkwardly toward the vases. "Thank you for bringing those," she added in a shaky voice.

I smiled again and nodded. She turned and walked briskly away.

I stayed a moment longer, gazing down at the little memorial, where the candle now shone out brightly in the deepening night. I wondered how often Rose Guild members came through the park. Would they see the vases and the candle, tomorrow, perhaps?

Turning away, I went to my car and drove home, thinking ahead to Tuesday. The tearoom would be open for business, the start of another work week. I'd have to make a follow-up call to the dairy about the cream, and I needed to put that quote together for Joan. Of course, the Rose Guild's plans might be changing—I'd have to wait and see.

The strange car was gone from behind the kitchen, and the lights were out. I parked in my usual spot and cast a glance toward the lilacs as I got out of the car. The garden was blessedly free of Goths. Thinking a silent thank-you to Ramon, I let myself into the house and went upstairs.

A light was on in my office. I paused, wondering if Captain Dusenberry was expanding his repertoire, then stepped in.

The light was my stained glass desk lamp, and it had been moved to illuminate a small dessert plate that sat in the center of my desk. I went around to sit in the desk chair, and saw that the plate held a perfect round of what looked like chocolate cake, one inch across and half an inch high, topped with a single fresh raspberry. In front of it sat a small envelope with my name on it in Julio's handwriting.

Dreading that it might be a letter of resignation, I opened the note.

Ellen -

This is from Adam. I brought him over to use the kitchen, but also because we needed to talk, not at home.

He got laid off and he's thinking about moving to California. I don't want him to go. If you gave him the assistant job it would give him some time to think about whether he really wants to leave.

My grandmother didn't approve of Adam. I think she really hated him, actually. So I hadn't seen her much in the last year or so. It's hard when you disagree with someone you love.

Anyway, thanks for understanding.

Julio

I laid the note on the desk. I was glad to know what was bothering Julio, but it raised a tricky question. Giving Adam a job would be kind, but it might also cause friction between him and Julio. How close were they? Maria's disapproval seemed to imply they were more than just roommates.

It was none of my business, of course. What Julio did on his own time was his concern. I just knew that mixing work and social life was rarely a good idea. I would have to talk with him, I suspected. A conversation that would probably be uncomfortable.

I picked up the confection and took a bite, then closed my eyes. What had looked like a simple chocolate cake was a torte, almost brownie-like, chewy with a hint of something herbal that I couldn't pinpoint. I had taken the topping for icing but it was ganache, creamy and rich with dark, dark chocolate. It set it off the torte perfectly, and the raspberry added a bright tang to the flavors.

This was not just a sweet, it was a work of art, as complex as a fine wine. Exactly the sort of thing I wanted for the tearoom.

OK, so Adam was a strong candidate. I still wanted to talk to Julio about whether they could work together without stressing their friendship.

I finished the torte and longed for another. I tucked Julio's note back into its envelope, then got up and carried the dessert plate with me out of the office

The candlesticks standing outside my suite caught me off guard. I stood gazing at them, then decided I didn't like them there. They didn't belong out in the hallway. They belonged in the suite, with my brocades and tasseled cords and the rest of my Renaissance decor.

Sighing, I let myself in, put the plate in the kitchenette, then went back and got one of the candlesticks and brought it into the suite. I looked all around the living room and kitchenette, but I'd tried every possible space there. They'd look ridiculous in the tiny bathroom. Turning to my right, I carried the candlestick into my bedroom.

My bed, a queen-sized canopy tricked out in rich brocades, is backed into a corner at an angle beneath the sloping roof. The flanking nightstands leave triangular spaces between the bed and the walls. I put the candlestick into one and set the candle on top, then fetched the other candlestick from the hall. Stepping back toward the chimney, I took in the effect.

They were perfect. Just the extra touch needed to make the bed look really luxurious. They were far enough from the canopy not to be a fire hazard, and out of traffic areas so they couldn't be knocked down or brushed against.

Maybe I'd known all along this was where they belonged. I just hadn't been ready to admit it.

I lit the candles and stood back. My bed glowed like a shrine. I smiled, wondering if that made me the offering. Then I blushed, and hastened to blow out the candles.

28

The next two days were a blur of activity. Rosa did not come in to work, by which I inferred that her family had been notified of Cora's arrest. Julio came in, worked silently and with frightening efficiency, and left early. I filled in for both of them as best I could, grateful that it was the slowest part of the week.

Slow is a relative term, however; Santa Fe's tourist season was in full swing and the tearoom saw a steady flow of new visitors. I divided my time between the kitchen, the butler's pantry, and the gift shop, with occasional forays upstairs to deal with the few business matters Kris couldn't resolve on her own.

By Wednesday afternoon, I was thinking longingly of margaritas and Ten Thousand Waves. I had just put a tray of frozen scones in the oven for the four o'clock seating, when the phone in the pantry rang.

"Ellen?" Kris said when I picked up. "There's a call for you on line two. Can you take it?"

"Let me get to the gift shop," I said, setting a timer for the scones.

Dee came in carrying an empty three-tiered food tray. She assured me she could handle the seated customers and wouldn't let the scones burn, and shooed me out of the pantry.

I walked forward to the gift shop, rang up a purchase for a young couple who were so plainly newly in love that I felt like showering them with rose petals, then picked up the waiting call.

"Ellen, it's Joan Timothy. I got your email with the quote for our annual event."

"Oh, yes. I'll understand if your plans have changed—"

"No, no. We're definitely coming! The menu is just what we were hoping for."

I thanked her and wrote down the date and her estimate of attendance. We would definitely have to put tables on the *portal*. We discussed a few more details, then fell into a brief silence.

I gazed out the window at the wisterias and cleared my throat. "You've—heard about Cora Young?"

"Oh, yes. We're having a special election to replace her," Joan said, a steely edge creeping into her voice. "Lucy Kingston, too—she's resigned."

"I'm so sorry."

"Don't be. I'm not. We'll be better off without them."

I couldn't help thinking that was true. I was searching for a tactful way to say so when my attention was distracted by the sight of the Bird Woman—wearing a red dress and long-fringed paisley shawl, with a turquoise scarf wrapped around her head—coming up the steps to the *portal* with Willow Lane. They were followed by a small troupe of elderly ladies in sun hats and shades.

"And I'd like to make a reservation for four next week," Joan said. "I'll be bringing our new officers to tea."

"Oh, yes! Just a moment." I glanced down at the reservation list, saw Mrs. Olavssen's name down for the dining parlor at four o'clock, and swallowed. I turned to the calendar and recorded Joan's request, by which time the ladies were out of my sight. I heard the tinkle of the bells on the front door.

"We'll send you an email to confirm," I told Joan. "Thanks so much."

After a hasty farewell, I stepped out into the hallway. The Bird Woman was halfway down it already, fringe dragging on the floor as she led her friends to the dining parlor. I hurried after them, catching up as they entered the parlor.

"So here's the Murder Room," the Bird Woman announced, accompanied by a jingling sound, "and Willow's going to tell us all about the murder that happened here. *Both* murders," she added, moving around to the far end of the table.

Willow took off her black straw hat and cast me an apologetic glance. I knew full well that this must be the Bird Woman's idea, not hers.

"May I take that for you?" I said.

"Thank you."

I took Willow's hat out to the hall and hung it on the coat rack, then escaped into the butler's pantry. Dee looked up from arranging sandwiches on a tiered food tray.

"Want me to serve them?" she asked, nodding toward the parlor.

I sighed with relief. "If you don't mind. I'll check on the other guests."

Dee dimpled. "I think she's kind of fun, but I know she gets on your nerves. This goes to Hyacinth," she said, handing me a cozy-covered teapot.

I spent the next hour in and out of the front parlors, the gift shop, the kitchen—anywhere but the dining parlor. Occasionally I heard the Bird Woman's stentorian tones, or Willow's lighter voice, drifting down the hallway. As six o'clock approached, I decided to ask Dee and Iz to handle closing the tearoom so I could prepare for the lecture that evening. I was just coming out of the pantry to look for Dee when the Bird Woman stepped out of the parlor. She raised her hands, and I realized the slight jingling I'd been hearing came from the large number of bangle bracelets she was wearing.

"There you are! I was afraid you weren't coming back!"

"We're a bit short-handed—"

She leaned toward me and lowered her voice slightly. "Thought I'd drum up some extra business for you. Willow told me about your tour package. I think I can get you a group from the Seniors Club every other week at least."

"How kind of you," I said, swallowing my pride.

"Anyway, I promised the girls they could meet you. Don't worry, it won't take a minute."

Resigning myself to fate, I followed her into the dining parlor, where her friends were happily chattering over the remains of their tea. They looked up at my entrance.

"This here's Ellen Rosings, the Mistress of the Tearoom," the Bird Woman said with a flourish and a jingle.

"Proprietress," I murmured, smiling. "I hope you all have enjoyed your tea."

They nodded and made affirmative noises. I backed toward the door.

"Oh, and before you go," the Bird Woman said, "we need a Ouija board. Do you have one?"

"I'm afraid not," I said faintly.

"Well, make sure you get one before the next tour. We're gonna need it to talk to Captain Dusenberry."

29

"It was interesting," Gina said, holding out her wineglass to be refilled, "but this one wasn't half as cool as the one about complex adaptive systems."

Tony, who was nearest the bottle, picked it up and poured. I watched his face, looking for a sign of approval or disapproval of the evening's entertainment, but he had on his neutral expression. I'd been wondering all night what was on his mind, and what had happened with Cora Young, but so far I hadn't had a chance to ask.

We'd rehashed the lecture over dinner, as Gina and I usually do. Alan, who was blond and wore an expression of indomitable optimism, had loved it. I suspected he would love anything Gina told him to love—he certainly seemed besotted with her.

Tony's comments had been more reserved, and I couldn't tell if he'd enjoyed himself or was just being polite. He had, however, given his complete attention to the lecture, which I thought indicated a genuine interest. It had been a good talk, though I agreed with Gina that I'd heard better.

"I thought it was great," Alan said for perhaps the third time. "That stuff about single-celled animals. That was really interesting!"

"Glad you liked it." Gina grinned, took a sip of her wine, and leaned over to kiss Alan's cheek. "Let's plan on going to next month's. All of us," she said, raising her glass toward me and Tony.

"What's the topic?" Tony asked.

Gina looked at me. I shrugged.

"I'll have to look it up. It's on their website."

"Well, let us all know the date so we can save it," Gina said.

I nodded, though I knew Tony couldn't commit absolutely, even if he wanted to. He could be called away to a crime scene at any time.

I also wasn't counting on Alan. He and Gina seemed pretty cozy now, but I knew that could also change in an instant. I hoped it wouldn't. He was nice, and I liked him better than I liked a lot of Gina's boyfriends. It would be more comfortable all around if he lasted a while.

We drifted to other topics as we polished off the last of the wine. The lighting at Pranzo was soft and warm. Tony's dark eyes reflected glints of candlelight. He'd worn a nice shirt and a silk tie, and looked rather splendid.

It was getting late, and no one wanted dessert. I was stifling yawns already; the last two days of frantic activity were catching up with me. Gina drove me and Tony back to my place and we all said goodbye, yes we must do it again, nice to meet you.

Tony walked me to the front door, through the garden rich with the scent of roses. I glanced at him sidelong as I took out my keys, still trying to figure out whether he'd enjoyed the evening, but I couldn't see his expression in the shade of the wisterias. I moved toward the door, into the glow of the porch lights flanking it.

"Nice dress," Tony said.

"Thanks."

"You really ought to go dancing in a dress like that."

I glanced down, caught a fold of the violet fabric in my hand. "Is that an invitation?"

"Yeah. How about Saturday?"

My heart jumped. "Sounds fun. I'll check my calendar and let you know."

"Okay."

He moved a step closer and I drew a sharp breath. "What happened with Cora Young?" I said, struck by a fit of chicken-heartedness.

Tony's face sobered a little. "She's going to be indicted. We got a warrant and searched her house. She had a jar of honey in her kitchen that matched the stuff on the rosebush she cut down. Minus the botulism, but the same honey."

"And the botulism? Did you find the source?"

"The clinic where she volunteers had a case about two weeks ago. That's where she got it. Someone there saw her slip a Petrie dish into her purse."

"Oh, how awful! Even though I know how she hated Maria, I can't believe she did it."

"People do awful things."

"Like cutting down perfectly good rosebushes."

"Actually, she did that out of compassion. After we got her to confess, she told us she cut down the rose because she was worried someone else would infect themselves. I guess she'd tried to clean the stuff off—"

"Yes, I watched her do it, though I didn't realize at the time that's what was going on."

"But she was worried she hadn't gotten it all. And she hadn't—there was enough left for us to identify."

I shook my head, saddened. "So she cut the rose down out of concern for her fellow human beings."

"Kind of ironic, since that's what led to her being caught."

I found the right key and unlocked the door. A yawn took me unawares and I apologized.

"Working too hard?" Tony said.

"I'm a little short-handed. I've been helping downstairs."

"Oh, yeah. When it rains it pours, eh?"

I shrugged, pushing open the door. "This is my career."

"Tea is your career?"

"Not just tea. Tea in a beautiful, peaceful place." I gestured toward the shadowed parlor. "Tea with dear friends, or with a good book, or with someone..."

My throat got tight, suddenly. I drew a sharp breath.

Tony nodded. "I get it. It's the atmosphere."

"Yes, exactly."

He stood watching me, and I couldn't decide whether to ask him in or not. If I did, would he expect me to take him upstairs? I wasn't ready for that, but I didn't want to completely discourage him.

"Well," he said.

I swallowed. Tony moved to step closer.

The hall lights came on. Tony looked up sharply.

"It's just Captain Dusenberry," I said. "This is a new one, he hasn't turned on the hall light before."

He frowned. "You don't really believe this place is haunted, do you?"

"Honestly, at this point I'm not sure what to believe."

Tony's eyes narrowed as he gazed down the hall. "Yeah. Want me to take a look around, just in case?"

"I don't think you'll find anything."

He gave me a flat look—the cop stare.

"Sure, go ahead," I said. Easier than arguing.

He stepped into the hall, moving slowly, listening. I followed, tiptoeing.

He edged his way up to the doorway of the main parlor, looking into it from the side. I couldn't help thinking of all the cop shows I'd seen on TV.

The stereo came on, cheerful strains of Mozart filling the tearoom.

"Crap," Tony muttered. "Where are the controls?"

"In the butler's pantry, but you won't—"

He was already halfway down the hall, moving with surprising silence. I stepped out of my shoes and hurried after him in my stocking feet.

I caught up with him at the door to the pantry, and saw that he had a gun in his hands. I stopped short, suddenly frightened. I hadn't even realized he was carrying a weapon.

He moved sideways along the wall toward the archway that led into the butler's pantry. I held my breath.

In one swift movement, Tony stepped into the pantry and brought his gun to chest height. I stayed where I was, though I could no longer see him.

"There's no one here," he said.

I let out my breath. "Right."

He stepped out into the hall, gun pointed at the floor, glaring at me. "If this is a joke—"

"I wouldn't dream of playing a prank like this on you. Honestly, Tony, I don't know what's doing it. I say it's Captain Dusenberry, but I don't know."

He turned to stare at the stereo. "Someone could rig up a remote control to turn that on."

"I guess."

"Same with the lights."

"Wouldn't they have to mess with the wiring?"

"Yeah."

"Well...I live here."

"They could wait until you go out."

I didn't like what he was suggesting. "There's been no sign of a break-in."

"Do you have an alarm system?"

"No..."

"Might want to get one."

I sighed. "I'll think about it."

"What's your email address? I'll send you some links to good shops."

I hesitated. Not that I didn't want Tony to have my email address, but it seemed kind of intimate. A friend thing, even though he was really just making a business recommendation.

I liked thinking of him as a friend.

I would have liked it more if he hadn't been holding a gun.

I opened my purse and took out a card, wrote my personal email on the back, and handed it to him. He shoved it in his back pocket, then looked at me, dark eyes concerned.

"Thanks. You going to be OK? Want me to check upstairs."

"There's no need, but thank you." I took a deep breath. "Tony, I have a request."

"Yeah?"

"I'd rather you didn't bring guns into the tearoom."

He stared at me, incredulous. "I always carry a gun."

"It's your job, I know. But do you think you could leave it at home when you're off duty?"

A frown settled on his brow. "A cop is never completely off duty. We're always watching."

"It's just that I'm trying to make this a place of peace. Guns don't fit into that."

"Then I guess I don't belong in your tearoom."

"Don't be angry, please."

He cast a restless look around the hallway. "I'm not, but you've got to understand. It's part of who I am."

I was sad at the thought that he couldn't bear to be apart from his weapon, even for a few hours. I swallowed.

"I do understand, but this is part of who *I* am," I said. "I want this house to be a place of harmony. I try to see the beauty in everyone I meet."

"I'm trained to see the ugly."

"I know."

Our gazes met, and the trouble in his beautiful, dark eyes made my heart ache. Maybe this wouldn't work, after all. Maybe we were too different.

"Just think about it, please," I whispered. "That's all I ask."

He sighed and nodded, then looked around the hallway. "All right. Call if you need me. Even if it's just Goths in the bushes."

I chuckled, relieved that he could still make a joke. "Thanks. Actually, you might be able to help me with that."

He turned his head toward me as we started toward the front door. "Oh?"

"I need to think about how to handle it. I'll let you know."

"OK. Oh, and thanks for the lecture," he said. "It was interesting."

"I'll email you the topic for the next one."

"Yeah."

We were at the door. Tony stood in front of it, glowering at it, then turned to me. "See you."

"See you."

A tiny frown creased his brow. With a swiftness that made me catch my breath, he leaned forward to kiss my cheek.

"Be safe."

He opened the door and went out, shutting it behind him.

"You, too," I said softly.

30

Candles glowed on the table in the dining parlor. I had brought out my mother's antique silver candelabra for the occasion, though I doubted Ramon and his friends appreciated them. Each held six candles, which lit the room fairly well. Tony's giant candle holders flanked the fireplace, and Willow stood in front of it, dressed in her black tour-guide style, talking about Captain Dusenberry to the Goths who were seated around the table.

"This room was the captain's study during his lifetime, and he was sitting at his desk here when he was murdered."

A flicker of interest showed in the face of the henna-haired girl, whose name was Alison. So far, the kids seemed unimpressed with the captain's history, but that might just be part of their brand of cool.

I glanced up at the chandelier. I had left it off, illuminating the room only with candlelight, both for atmosphere and in the hope that Captain Dusenberry might indulge my guests by turning it on. So far, nothing—not even a wiggling crystal.

"The murderer stood in the doorway and shot the captain twice, hitting him in the back and the head. He was found the next morning by his servant, Private David Rogers. Nothing was taken from the house, and the killer was never caught."

Thea, an androgynous, painfully thin girl with spiky black hair hanging in her eyes, raised her hand. "How long did he take to die? Did he, like, suffer a lot?"

"Probably not," Willow said. "He was still in his chair, fallen forward onto his desk, when he was found. It's likely that he was unconscious, if not dead, immediately."

"So he didn't leave a last message or anything?"

Scrawled in blood, perhaps? I kept the thought to myself.

"No," Willow said. "He'd been working on an inventory report. It was found on the desk beneath his body."

Ramon raised his hand. "What part of the room was the desk in?"

"That's not known, but I would guess that it was about where Ms. Rosings is standing."

I started, and took a step to one side. Willow was probably right—if I were to use the room as a study, I would place my desk so that I could see both the door and the windows.

"Have you ever seen him?" asked a third girl...Wendy? Mindy?

"I have not, but I do get a sense of his presence in the house, and in this room particularly," Willow said.

The kids looked around the room, as if to spot Captain Dusenberry hovering in a corner. I wondered if it was time to bring out the tea and scones. Julio had made some blood orange curd especially for this group.

A creak sounded above our heads. Everyone looked up at the ceiling. The chandelier was motionless.

A slow, heavy tread moved across the ceiling, then descended the stairs. The kids exchanged glances, eyes wide with excitement. Their faces turned toward the door as the footsteps came down the hall.

A man appeared in the shadowed doorway, wearing the dark blue uniform of a mid-nineteenth-century army officer. His hat—a forage cap, I'd been told—was pulled down so that the bill hid his eyes.

"Boo," he said.

The kids laughed.

"You're not a ghost!" Alison accused.

"No, I'm not," Tony said, stepping into the dining parlor. "But we thought you might like to see the kind of uniform

Captain Dusenberry would have worn, and the kind of gun that killed him."

He took a Colt Navy pistol—a replica, though it looked like an antique—from the holster at his hip. The kids gathered around him.

"Cool!"

"Is it loaded?"

Tony glanced at me. "No. It's a black powder weapon. It gets loaded with a cartridge like this one."

He took a paper cartridge and a loose bullet from his pocket and showed them to the kids, demonstrating how the gun would be loaded but not actually doing so. We had agreed on that, and he stuck to his word.

The gun was plainly the highlight of the evening for the kids, though Ramon took an interest in the officer's sword Tony also wore. Tony had borrowed the uniform and weapons from a friend on the police force who was a Civil War reenactor.

I suppressed a small sigh as I slipped out to fetch the tea and scones. So much for peace and harmony. These Goth kids wanted murder and mayhem.

But maybe they'd like the scones, and maybe one or two of them would come back for tea sometime, and get an idea that beauty and elegance could also be cool. I could hope.

I had also told Ramon I was serious about hiring him to come play guitar at the tearoom, once a week through the summer, until he had to go back to college. I was all for encouraging talent, and it might give him a new focus for his energies.

I served tea and scones while the kids continued to pepper Tony with questions, many of them unanswerable. Willow offered explanations where she could, but the fact remained that very little was known about Captain Dusenberry's murder. I had made an appointment to go to the museum with

Willow and talk to her friend, who I hoped could shed some light on the matter, or at least point me toward more information. The captain's unsolved murder was becoming a mission for me.

When the scones had all been devoured, Willow made some closing remarks, and I wished Ramon and his friends good night. Tony helped me usher them out the back door. Ramon hung back.

"Thanks, Ms. Rosings," he said, smiling. "It was really interesting."

"I'm glad you enjoyed it."

He looked at Tony and held up his hand for a fist-bump, then shepherded his friends toward their cars. I watched them pile in and drive away.

"Well, that's that," I said, going through the French doors back into the dining parlor. "Hopefully they'll come in the front door from now on, if they come back at all."

"I'm going to go change out of this wool," Tony said.

"Hot?" I asked.

"Itchy. Ray offered to lend me some long johns to wear underneath, but I said nah. Now I wish I'd taken him up on it."

"You'll have to do that if we make this presentation again," Willow said.

"Hm." Tony headed upstairs without further comment.

I turned to Willow. "There's a little tea left. Would you like some?"

"No, thanks. It'll keep me awake."

"I could make some tisane..."

"No, I ought to be going. This went well, Ellen. Would Tony be willing to present the Captain again, do you think?"

"I don't know."

"If not, perhaps his friend could put us in touch with one of the reenactors. I could see making this a part of our tour-and-tea package."

"I'll ask him," I said. "Thanks again, Willow." I handed her an envelope containing a thank-you note and a gift card for tea for two.

"My pleasure," she said, gazing at the chandelier.

One crystal was swinging gently back and forth, glinting in the candlelight.

Willow looked at me sidelong and smiled. "Good night," she said softly.

I saw her out, then turned on the chandelier. The brilliance of electricity made me blink. I began putting out the candles, using my mother's candle extinguisher, smiling at the memory of her teaching me how much better it was than blowing candles out. No wax flying onto your table, and besides, it was more elegant.

The evening had gone well, and I was grateful. There'd been constraint between me and Tony ever since our talk about guns. We hadn't gone dancing; this was the first I'd seen of him since the evening of the lecture, though we'd exchanged emails. It felt as if we'd taken a step back in our friendship, but at least we were still talking.

Tony came downstairs, wearing a dark t-shirt and jeans, his arms piled with the uniform and accoutrements. I picked up another envelope and walked out with him to the back. He'd driven his mother's car, since the uniform and weapons were too much to carry on his bike. I waited until he'd loaded them in, then handed him the envelope.

"What's this?"

"A gift card. I thought you might like to bring your grandmother to tea."

"That's nice of you. I'll have to warn her she can't smoke here."

"I'd appreciate that."

His lips twitched. "She might say no. She loves her cigs."

"Well, then maybe you could bring your mother, or one of your sisters."

"Yeah." He looked down at the envelope, held between his hands. The paper made a small crinkling sound. He looked up at me.

"Would you join us?"

Heart skip. "I'd be honored," I said.

He nodded, then turned and tossed the envelope onto the passenger seat. "Well."

"Thanks for doing this," I said. "You were the hit of the evening. Willow wants to know if you'd do it again."

He grimaced. "I don't know."

"Or if not, whether Ray could recommend someone."

"That's probably a better way to go. Those kids asked a lot of questions I couldn't answer. A real Civil War buff wouldn't look so dumb."

"You didn't look dumb. You looked rather handsome, I thought."

"Yeah?"

"In a macho, gun-toting sort of way."

He laughed softly, shaking his head. "Right. OK, good night."

"Good night, Tony. Thanks again."

"Glad to help."

He got in and started the engine.

"The door is ajar," said the car.

I pushed it closed and Tony hastily buckled his seat belt, then rolled down the window. "I'll call you."

"OK."

He stared at me for a few seconds, then gave a little chin-lift and backed the car. I retreated to the dining parlor and stood watching him through the French doors.

The chandelier went out.

I stayed where I was, better able to see Tony as I stood in

the darkened parlor. I wondered if he had noticed the light going out. If he had, he didn't let it stop him.

Ellen's Rose Petal Jam

Note: Harvest roses from bushes that have not been sprayed or treated with systemic insecticide, or use edible rose petals from a commercial source. If you harvest your own roses, cut them in the late morning. Wash them on the stem, being careful of any thorns. Gather the petals into a bud with your fingertips and pull from the stem, then use scissors to clip off the white bases, which are bitter. Wash the petals again, thoroughly.

Ingredients

1 cup fresh edible rose petals
2 cups sugar
4 cups water
2 lemons
fruit pectin (optional)
1/2 T cold butter

Put rose petals into a bowl and sprinkle with 1 cup sugar. Toss with your fingers, bruising petals to release their fragrance. Cover bowl with plastic wrap and refrigerate overnight.

Juice the lemons, leaving any seeds in the juice (for pectin). In medium saucepan, combine lemon juice, seeds, water, and remaining sugar (1 cup). Add a little fruit pectin if desired. Heat gently, stirring until sugar is dissolved. Add rose petals and simmer 20 minutes, stirring occasionally. Bring to a boil and cook for 5 minutes* until jam thickens (220°F or 105°C), or until a spoonful dropped onto a cold plate shows jam texture.

Remove from heat. Stir in butter. Use a spoon to remove lemon seeds.

Pour jam into clean jars, close lids tightly. Use hot water bath if you like, or just store in refrigerator after cooling.

Note—at elevations over a mile above sea level this may take much longer, up to half an hour. This has an added benefit: you may end up cleaning your kitchen while you wait for the jam to thicken.

About the Author

Patrice Greenwood was born and raised in New Mexico, and remembers when dusty dogs rolled in the Santa Fe plaza. She loves afternoon tea, old buildings, gourmet tailgating at the opera, and solving puzzles.

Books by Patrice Greenwood

Wysteria Tearoom Mysteries

A Fatal Twist of Lemon
A Sprig of Blossomed Thorn

Made in the USA
Lexington, KY
12 April 2015